THE ISSUE

IN OAKTOWN

Renay Jackson

BRIDGETTE,
ENJOY THE
BOOK SISTER !

THE ISSUE IN OAKTOWN
Copyright © 2016
Renay Jackson

Distributed by: J-MAC 2 Publishing
900 N. La Brea Avenue, Suite 154
Inglewood, Ca. 90302
Jmac2publishing@gmail.com

Cover Design By: Nalon
artsynalon@gmail.com

Edited By: Professional Publishing House
www.professionalpublishinghouse.com
Library of Congress Catalog-in-Publication Data

Jackson, Renay, 1959-
        The Issue in Oaktown / Renay Jackson
        p. cm.

ISBN: 978-0-9981679-0-9

Printed in the United States by Morris Publishing®
3212 East Highway 30
Kearney, NE 68847
1-800-650-7888

DEDICATIONS

This book is dedicated to all of the young men eighteen and under in my family. I pray that Fathers, Grandfathers, Uncles, Teachers, Preachers, and Coaches assist in sharing with you the realities of the world we live in.

Schooling you on the hard lessons in life they have learned to navigate and how to deal with friends, enemies, & the police.

My Grandson
Jelani Elijah Antonio Belvine

My Great Nephews
Elijah Blankenship
Jahmon Harvey-Cooper Jr.
Levigne & Leighton Proctor-Draquez
Yusuef Ettlinger
Aljon, Allen, Cyrus, Elijah, Jabri & Sean Foster
Jalen, Jordan, Taj, & Shawn Henderson Jr.
Kamal Jabari
Reneaux, Raylio, and Kanai Jackson
Tyrone Blair Ratliff
Heru Richmond

To everyone else in the family – I Love You All.
To the Lord GOD Almighty – Thank You for blessing me. I give You all the glory.

OTHER NOVELS BY RENAY JACKSON

Oaktown Devil

Shakey's Loose

Turf War

Peanut's Revenge

Crack City

Sweetpea's Secret

PROLOGUE

"Can I say something Coach?" D-Money cut in.

"By all means, Demonte." Mister Tucker spread his arms in a sweeping motion across the room "the floor is all yours" he sat down as D-Money stood up.

"I mean not to defend police, but in most of those cases you named, black men were breaking the law. It seems to me like they should have Black Lives Matter when we kill each other. You had two people shot at the Sydeshow Friday night with hundreds of folks there, yet nobody stepped up to say they saw it."

Before D-Money could sit down, Venitra shot out of her seat like a cannon.

"How dare you say that, Demonte?" she screamed. "You should be ashamed to call yourself a black man. Our brothers are out there killing each other because the system is set up that way. They can't get no jobs, locked in prison all their life for petty crimes, have to work twice as hard just to get half as much as whites do" she was once again slapping her right backhand into her left palm "I don't care what they were doing, that doesn't give the police the right to kill them. It could be your brother, cousin, father, uncle, or even your son if you ever have one. I'm ashamed of you." Levitra went to a seat on the other side of the room, glaring menacingly at D-Money as she sat down.

"See that's what I mean," Demonte said.

"Okay," Mister Tucker cut in. "Jeff, you've been quiet."

"The way I see it," JP said, "is All Lives Matter. Cops killing blacks, blacks killing cops, it's all wrong but that doesn't give you the right to blame it on whites Venitra, or say stuff like you have to work twice as hard to get half as much as we do."

Venitra stood up, but Mister Tucker motioned for her to sit down, so JP continued.

"You need to check your history when you begin talking about the past because if you did, you would know that slavery began with blacks selling other blacks to the white man for money."

"Wait a minute, JP." Lavelle finally spoke up "how could blacks sell blacks to the white man when they spoke different languages?"

"Check your history, Lavelle," JP responded. "It's a fact."

"Is that what they tell you in the suburbs?" Octavia asked as if she couldn't believe what she had heard

"No stereotyping, Miss Wilson," Tucker admonished.

Octavia Wilson had the build of a track star, which she just so happened to be. With a skin complexion as yellow as buttered popcorn, she favored bright red lipstick painted on delicious mouth-watering lips. Sporting a gold dyed short curly afro, she was blessed with curves in all the right places. The girl was super fine.

"Oh, my bad, Mister Tucker," she said. "What you have to understand, Jeffrey, is that whites steal everything we have."

"What have they stole?" He didn't know where she was headed with that statement.

"They steal our lips, they steal our butts, they steal our music, they steal our dance, they want our men and the men want our women. Then to top it off, they feel threatened by us so they resort to stereotyping our brothers, fathers, cousins, uncles, and sons as lazy and dangerous. Of course, you wouldn't understand because you have what is known as white privilege." she snapped her finger and swiveled her head.

"White privilege," JP reasoned. "I'm not privy to anything."

"Privy" she mocked "you don't get followed around in stores simply for being white. You don't get the maximum sentence for doing the minimum crime, passed over for jobs when you're the most qualified candidate, denied promotions or raises, have people go to the other side of the street because they see you coming towards them ..."

"That has nothing to do with what we're talking about, Octavia, and you know it." JP interrupted her sermon.

- "Gavin Long, black, of Kansas City ambushed white cops in Louisiana."

- "Micah Xavier Johnson, black, ambushed cops in Texas."

- "Lovelle Mixon, black, ambushed cops right here in this city."

"So what you're telling me is that those murders were justified?" he questioned.

"Dude, you don't get it," she said.

"Okay, everyone." Mister Tucker spoke. "For the remainder of class we will break off into groups of four to discuss these issues. I need one person in each group to record the ideas and statements made. I would also like you to select a spokesperson for your group."

The class was now alive with sidebar conversations going on throughout the room. Many who entered as friends would now leave as foes.

THE ISSUE
IN OAKTOWN

AUTHOR'S NOTE

This book is based totally on the writer's imagination. Any similarities to actual events are purely coincidental. Although many of the locations are real, they were used only to make the story believable.

TABLE OF CONTENTS

1	THE FUTURE	1
2	MADNESS	17
3	FIVE-O	29
4	BAD ATTITUDE	37
5	PAYBACK	53
6	FAMILIAR SCENE	61
7	MAMA DRAMA	67
8	THE DISCUSSION	75
9	PARTNERS	95
10	THE HOLDUP	99
11	MAKEUP	103
12	THE ASSIGNMENT	113
13	INTERROGATED	117
14	OPPOSING SIDES	125
15	ISSUES	133
16	THUGS	141
17	TOWN HALL	147
18	CONSEQUENCES	157
19	RETRIBUTION	161

TABLE OF CONTENTS *(cont)*

20	INEVITABLE	165
21	THE CHASE	169
22	HOMEWORK	173
23	INTERNAL INVESTIGATION	185
24	GRAND JURY	195
25	AT IT AGAIN	199
26	SUMMER JOB PROGRAM	203
27	REST IN PEACE	209
28	NEW DETECTIVES	213
29	CHANGE IS COMING	217
30	FOOT IN MOUTH	221
	EPILOGUE	227

THE FUTURE

As the clock neared three-fifteen, students anxiously eyed it watching the seconds slowly tick away. It had been a very long week and for most, the weekend couldn't arrive fast enough. The bell sounded and chaos took over as everyone made a mad dash for the door. Robert Garcia slowly put away books inside his backpack smiling as his three homeboys did the same. They had been friends since grade school and were as thick as thieves. Once done, the foursome headed for the exit.

It had been an unusually hot month of April with record breaking temperatures on a daily basis. Bobby, as he was called by everyone, loved it because it allowed him the opportunity to wear form fitting shirts, which displayed his muscular physique. A star athlete, he played wide receiver in football and point guard on the basketball teams.

With high school nearing an end, Bobby eagerly anticipated the next chapter in his life. He had big dreams and was determined to make them realities. Standing five feet ten inches on a solid hundred and eighty-five-pound frame, he had been told by college recruiters that he was not tall enough to play division one in football as a wide receiver or hoops as a point guard. The recommendation from them was for him to try and land a division two scholarship but Bobby was having none of that and dismissed the thought.

Since his grades were excellent, he was going to a D-1 school on an academic scholarship and would prove the so- called experts wrong by trying out as a walk-on, then excelling as he had done on every level. Built solid like a Mack truck, Bobby had jet black hair, which was always neatly trimmed. His brown, almond-shaped face displayed a baby mustache under his chin, and dark black steely eyes that could bore in on you like a laser beam.

"Man," he spoke to the crew, "let's go get a shake."

"I'm down with that," responded D-Money.

"All righty then," Bobby said, "milkshakes it is." Bobby slapped a handshake with D-Money as they headed for the parking lot. Those two grew up living next door to each other and acted more like brothers than friends. The fact that Bobby was Mexican and D-Money black was irrelevant. When it came to those two, color didn't matter. They had similar interests in girls, fashion, hobbies, and dreams of the good life.

Demonte Edwards, or D-Money as he was known, had just as much talent as Bobby, but he had his own set of issues preventing him from gaining a D-1 athletic scholarship, too. Just like Bobby, he made excellent grades in the classroom, so college on an academic scholarship was also in his future plans. At six foot one, his height was not the problem as a defensive back in football. He possessed cat-like quickness and a nose for the ball. However, his skinny, one hundred and sixty-five-pound body scared recruiters away, who felt he was a concussion waiting to happen.

D-Money was handsome. His milk chocolate complexion accented by high cheekbones, soft brown eyes, pearl white teeth, and a medium-sized round nose on a lean angular face. An impeccable dresser, he was always sharp, flossing the latest fashions. The greatest attribute he possessed was his laid back demeanor which endeared him to all throughout the campus.

On the basketball court he was a sharp shooting marksman who could light it up from anywhere. However, recruiters felt his defense was weak and his six-one height would be a problem against bigger shooting guards. They also felt that unless he packed on some pounds, he would be pushed around under the boards. D-Money could care less about any of it because he was focused on getting an education and using his brain instead of his athletic talent to get noticed.

D-Money and Bobby arrived at the vehicle, then turned around to see what was taking their boys so long. Bobby, easily irritated, was visibly upset at the delay because Lavelle and JP were casually strolling through the parking lot conversing with a crowd of females.

"Man, come on," he shouted. "We're going to be last in line."

"Calm down, Bobby…. It's not like they will run out of food." JP belted out a laugh.

"Or shakes," chimed in Lavelle.

"Oh, you got jokes now?" Bobby said to Lavelle while getting into the back seat. "Don't let the success get to your head, Bro."

"You're the one," Lavelle answered. "Win one championship and now you walk around in muscle shirts like a prima donna."

Everyone laughed at that joke, including Bobby, while JP slowly eased his vehicle through the crowd of both girls and boys who were waving as they passed. They all had been on a natural high since surprising everyone one month earlier by winning the state open division basketball championship. In the Northern California title game, they defeated perennial powerhouse De La Salle, topping the mighty Spartans in an overtime nail-biter.

The state championship game was another nip-and-tuck thriller against the number two, nationally ranked Long Beach Poly Jackrabbits. The win was secured on a last second, three-pointer by Lavelle, who was immediately hoisted into the air by delirious teammates and carried off the court. The victory served as the punctuation mark to a magical season in which their only loss was to eventual national champion, DeMatha High, of Maryland, in a Christmas holiday tournament featuring several of the nation's best high school squads.

It was that week in Vegas where the team realized they were special and could compete against anyone. Lavelle Brookins, a high school, all-American, was the focal point of the team and stood six-feet eight inches tall on a powerful Dwight Howard type two-hundred and forty-pound frame. He had already accepted a scholarship from the University of Kentucky where he would be joining four other All-Americans to replace five underclass teammates departing early for the riches of the NBA.

Although he possessed a man-child body, his face resembled that of a still growing seventeen-year-old kid. Lavelle had average-sized lips, a small pointy nose, and hazel eyes on an oval-shaped face, which was topped off by short and wavy brown hair. With a black father and white mother, he was often mistaken for white by opposing coaches, players, and fans.

This oversight did not bother him in the least because at his school alone, there were interracial students all over campus. It was nothing out of the ordinary to see mixed race couples in serious puppy love relationships. Same sex lovers, too, for that matter. So to Lavelle, the mixed race would one day eventually become the dominant race in America.

"Well, would you look at that," JP said humorously. "The parking lots empty."

"You know mister prima donna can't be told anything nowadays," Lavelle said.

"Aw, man, forget you two clowns," Bobby sneered. "Just jealous because I don't have to be on a diet plan."

"Unless you slow it down, you'll be fat, Bro," Lavelle seriously said. "Junk food is not cool."

"*Junk food is not cool,*" Bobby mimicked sarcastically

"Bobby, you really need to pay attention to
what you're shoving into your body"
chipped in JP "that stuff will lead to all kind
of medical complications down the road"
"Yeah, whatever." Bobby dismissed the
comment.

"Good Eats" sat across the street from the
Foothill Square shopping center on the corner of
107th & MacArthur. Over the years it had changed
ownership and menus numerous times from a
burger joint, to a chicken shack, then a pizzeria, and
a fish spot. Now owned by an Asian couple, the
food faire was burgers, Mexican, Chinese, or
sandwiches, along with shakes, ice cream, and chili
fries. A popular hangout for high school kids, Good
Eats, was the after-school place to be.

JP pulled his ten-year old 4Runner into an
empty stall of the sparsely occupied parking lot and
the foursome got out and went inside. The vehicle
was silver in color and in mint condition. It had
been a gift to him on his sixteenth birthday from his
father and served its purpose very well. First, it
provided enough leg room for him to ride
comfortably. It also made getting to school easy by
not having to rely on his parents or public
transportation to get there.

Jeffrey Peters IV came from a long line of
doctors and was determined to keep up the family
tradition. The comment to Bobby about eating
habits was just the future doctor within him. Super
smart in the classroom, he also excelled on the
basketball court but that success was mired in
controversy.

He lived in the Tri-Valley suburb of San Ramon, yet convinced his parents that he should attend an inner city school for his senior year in order to improve his understanding of different cultures. Besides, JP felt as though he could not win a state title being the focal point of his team's offense. He fashioned himself as a complimentary player and had no qualms with Lavelle being the star. Neither he nor his parents were prepared for the backlash they would receive from such a personal decision regarding his future.

Upon learning of his intentions to transfer to a rival school for no legitimate reason, all of his teammates stopped speaking to him. Everyone he knew for that matter ignored him. When he saw a familiar face inside the grocery store or shopping mall, be it boy or girl, they would turn away and avoid all contact with him. JP was considered a traitor within his own community and was no longer welcome in San Ramon. Former friends would openly state that he should move to that crummy city, so he could be around "those people" all the time.

JP didn't care because it was his decision alone and no one could tell him how to live his life. A free spirit, he stood six-eleven on a rather thin two hundred and sixty-pound frame yet was a relentless rebounder. JP also had a nice midrange game to complement his feathery shooting touch. His favorite shot was a fade away jumper that could not be blocked due to his height. Paired up with Lavelle Brookins, they presented opponents with an imposing front line very difficult to defend.

He had blond hair, which flowed just past the shoulders to mid-back. He wore it in a ponytail secured by a rubber band and always covered by a baseball cap. Aqua blue eyes, a long nose, and thin lips complemented his golden boy look. JP loved his new school, new environment, and new friends. The state championship reinforced his belief that he had made the right decision.

Inside the diner, the group ordered their food then sat down at a table looking out onto the street. Their conversation, which been filled with braggadocio and playful putdowns, now took on a serious nature.

"Man, I still can't believe it. First in my family to go to college," said Bobby.

"Where you going?" asked D-Money.

"Fresno State," Bobby responded. "Close, but far enough away."

"Are you playing ball?" D-Money probed.

"You know it, the basketball coach said I can walk on and be given a fair shot at making the team. That's all I can ask for, a chance to compete."

"True dat," D-Money said. "Seems fair enough, long as they keep their word."

"They'd better," Bobby growled, "or else they're going to have a problem. Where you headed?"

"Boise State," D-Money stated.

"Boise State." Lavelle coughed up some fries. "Man, what you know about Idaho? That they make potatoes?" Lavelle, JP, and Bobby roared with laughter.

"Same thing you know about Kentucky," D-Money deadpanned. "NOTHING."
Now the group laughed at Lavelle so D-Money continued, "I'm getting as far away from this madness as I can."
"I hate to be the one to tell you, Bro, but madness is everywhere," Bobby said.
"Not in Boise, dude. It's nice and quiet."
"I always thought you were a city slicker," JP said,
"I am, but I can fit in anywhere."
"Wow, just think," JP continued. "In a few months, we will all be headed our separate ways."
"I do think of it," Bobby chipped in. "That's crazy."
"Well, since no one bothered to inquire as to my college choice, I'll just be quiet," JP stated.
"Awwww, Baby's feelings get hurt?" Bobby teased.
"We didn't mean to overlook you, Boo," D-Money cracked.
"Man, it's not a secret," said Lavelle.
"Everybody knows you're going to Stanford and follow in your parent's footsteps, Doctor Peters," the group roared,
"Actually, I've changed my mind and am going to Cal."
"CAL?" they all shouted. "What did your father say?" Lavelle asked.
"I have not told them yet," JP answered.
"I'm sure they'll be pissed, especially Dad,

but he will just have to get over it. This is my life. I plan on double majoring in Political Science and Medicine."

"I thought Stanford and the Silicon Valley were your plans," Lavelle said before continuing. "What changed your mind?"

"Velle, you are wayyyy off base." Bobby spoke out of turn. "JP wants to go into politics so he can legally cheat folks out of their money. Look at him. He's the right color, got a handsome face, can lie his ass off...." They all erupted with laughter.

"Lie," JP responded. "That's what the campaign manager is for." He paused for emphasis. "And we all know Bobby will be my campaign manager." Now they all laughed at Bobby.

"Go to hell, JP, and take that one move with you," Bobby chided.

D-Money noticed several cars pulling into the Foothill Square parking lot across the street. With darkness rapidly approaching, he knew these were early revelers for the Sydeshow seeking prime front row spots for the madness soon to occur. Not wanting any part of it, he addressed the crew.

"Man, we better get out of here before that madness I was talking about jumps off."

The rest of them noticed and promptly put their food scraps into the trash can, placing the serving treys on top of the receptacle. Outside, they relished the fresh breeze, which slapped them in their faces. Before they had a chance to get inside the 4Runner, a group of people approached.

"Looka here, looka here .... The neighborhood squares," said Taco.

"Ignore him," Lavelle whispered into JP's ear.

"Hey, boy, you hear me talking to you?" He moved towards them.

"Look, Bro, we don't want no trouble," said Lavelle.

"Trouble hell." He took a swig of liquor. "Thank y'all sumptun 'cause y'all play basketball fa dat lame coach, huh? I'm better than all y'all put together." He noticed D-Money looking past him. "What you lookin at, fool? That's my woman."

"You know we know who she is," said D-Money as he got into the back seat.

"Honey, leave them alone," said Synnetra. "Let's go have some fun."

JP drove off with Taco spewing profanities at them as they entered traffic.

"Who is that guy?" asked JP.

"We call him Taco," D-Money answered.

"That's his name? JP responded with another question.

"That's his street tag," said Lavelle before continuing. "He used to ball with us until he got popped."

"You mean jail?" JP responded with yet another question.

"Yea, man, jail," said D-Money from the back seat. "He was pretty good, but wanted fast money and thought slangin was the way to get it. The reason he's mad at Coach is because Coach would always try to tell him dealing drugs was not the way to go. Somehow, he blamed Coach for his troubles."

"He also was a ball hog and an alcoholic," shot Bobby. "Wanted to play street ball and be the star instead of running the designed plays."

"So I take it he played your position?" JP kept the questions coming.

"Man, that fool can't out ball me," Bobby responded angrily. "Matter of fact, he can't even read."

"They just let him out last week, but he knows what we did," stated D-Money. "I guess he's just jealous."

"That explains why he said he was better than all of us put together. Incredible," said JP.
At that moment, police lights came on with the siren blaring.

"What are they doing?" J.P spoke out loud while pulling over. "I've done nothing wrong."

"Pull out your driver's license and sit it on the dashboard," said D-Money.

"Wrists on the steering wheel, fingers spread out," shouted Bobby.

"Answer 'yes sir, no sir'; to all questions," D-Money warned.

"Here's your proof of insurance." Lavelle handed him the insurance card from the glove box. "Put it with your license and make no direct eye contact."

"What are you guys doing?" JP asked, not understanding their actions.

JP could not comprehend the sudden change that had overcome his friends. They all seemed paranoid for no reason what so ever; it was simply a traffic stop. Letting out a whoosh of air, he tugged down on his baseball cap.

"Man, put your hands on the steering wheel," Lavelle stated forcefully.

Before JP could respond, an officer stepped up to his driver side window with a hand on his service revolver. His partner flashed a light into the passenger side, hand on his weapon, also while peering inside at the vehicle's occupants.

"Where you boys coming from?" asked the cop whose eyes were now focused on Bobby and D-Money in the back seat

"We got something to eat after school," answered JP.

"Wouldn't be a part of that Sydeshow gathering, would you?" asked the cop.

"No, Sir, Officer Haskins" JP answered noticing the name on his uniform.

Officer Haskins saw that all four teens had their hands in plain view and since the two occupants in front were white, he would end this patrol stop.

"Looks like your tail light might be malfunctioning. You should get it checked."

"Yes, Sir," JP said dryly.

Haskins and his partner returned to their squad car and drove off. JP sat there with his hands still clutching the steering wheel, trying to figure in his brain what had just happened. The moment the cop car pulled away, JP got out of his vehicle to check his tail lights.

"I knew it!" he screamed. "There's nothing wrong with my tail lights."

"I don't even see why you checked," said D-Money.

"Man, what just happened here?" JP asked to no one in particular.

"It's called being black or brown," Bobby answered. "In your world it's referred to as profiling and, until now, something you have never had to go through."

"See. It's something we're taught at a young age," D-Money chipped in. "Before you reach to get your license, you'd better ask them if you can get it out of your pocket."

"And then move super slowly while you do it," said Lavelle.

"It could be the difference between life and death," stated Bobby.

"Now with your license and insurance already out, hands in clear view holding the steering wheel, the only reason he would have to clown was if you acted stupid or defied his commands," said Lavelle.

"Are you serious?" JP was stunned. "I've heard this kind of stuff goes on, but never witnessed it firsthand. That was eerie. We were basically stopped for no reason."

"JP, my man, welcome to our world," said D-Money before continuing, "I would, however, like to thank you because you just saved us."

"Saved you? What are talking about?"

"When that cop looked in here and saw the future Governor of California sitting behind the wheel, he knew what time it was." They all laughed. "We didn't even have to turn on the dome light." They laughed again even louder.

"Very funny, ha, ha," JP sourly commented. "Man, you think we're not nervous from that crap?" D-Money stated. "What most white people don't know is the Po-Po be on serious edge, man. They play right into that black thug stereotype and are so antsy that if you move wrong … BANG, BANG, you're dead."

"So we always have to be on point when it comes to dealing with five-o, see what I'm saying?" Lavelle added more of a fact than a question.

They rode the rest of the way in silence, listening to music, as each one drifted off into their own thoughts.

2

MADNESS

With the explosion of social media, a weekly gathering, known as the "Sydeshow," aided teens and young adults in outsmarting the cops. By the time five-o, or the Po Po, as cops were disdainfully called, would figure out the codes from Facebook, Twitter, or Instagram, young hoodlums had devised another method in letting everyone know when and where the event would be held.

The best estimate of when the Sydeshow originated was the mid-nineties and it was anyone's guess as to where it started. Oaktown, just like Los Angeles and numerous other cities across the country, took credit for its birth. No one could prove where it all actually began. However, one thing was certain, the Sydeshow posed a weekly problem for law enforcement agencies.

Thousands of people would receive text messages, emails, or posts on their social media accounts, informing them of the night's location and activities. Usually held on weekends, participants converged on a main intersection blocking off dozens of city streets which prevented the police from getting anywhere near the festivities.

Arriving from all counties, which included San Francisco, Alameda, Solano, San Mateo, San Joaquin, and Contra Costa, along with far away locales like Sacramento and San Jose, the Sydeshow proved to be too large of an event for local cops to manage. They were simply outnumbered by the huge mass of revelers participating in the madness.

Chaos reigned supreme with all businesses except liquor stores, which were plentiful. Fast food eateries and gas stations shut down the moment they realized what was going on. Residents locked themselves inside their homes like prisoners while their yards were trampled, sexual acts took place openly and people urinated or defecated on their property. The teens and adults also did drugs, got drunk, engaged in fistfights, gambled, broke into cars, and destroyed property.

The main attraction would occur on numerous intersections simultaneously where people would form human circles with a car in the center. The car would proceed to do "doughnuts," spinning its wheels wildly as drivers displayed their skills. It was a maneuver picked up from NASCAR drivers who, after winning a race, would spin their car in a circular motion by hitting both the gas and brake pedals at the same time.

With music playing so loud it would shake the ground, drivers hit doughnuts, filling the air with so much smoke you could barely see in front of yourself. The stunts were terrifying because cars would come so close to people who formed the circle so that many had to dive out of the way to avoid being hit. For the unfortunate soul that did strike a pedestrian, they were yanked out of their car and severely beaten by an angry mob for not knowing how to drive.

Another dangerous aspect was that fools would hang out of open doors while the car was spinning, sit on top of the hood, or play matador, as if the car were a bull. Of course, people were injured routinely and many even lost their life while attending these events, yet the madness flourished.

To combat the problem, every available police officer would be required to work overtime on weekends, effectively putting a serious dent in the city budget. Neighboring agencies along with the Highway Patrol and Sheriff's Department would also provide assistance. To recoup some of the financial loss, cars were impounded for expired tags, malfunctioning turn signals, and busted lights. People were arrested on the spot for invalid or expired licenses, drunk driving, being intoxicated in public, possession of drugs or weapons, and fighting. Tow truck operators were busy hauling away cars as fast as they possibly could and since the city jail was closed due to budget cuts, the county jail would be overflowing with people awaiting their day in court, locked up until the next business day. That would be on Monday, or Tuesday if it was a holiday weekend.

On Monday morning, the line on the third floor of the police station Records Department stretched down the stairs to the first floor and outside the front door to the street. Numerous excuses, or reasons, were given to the clerks as to why the steep fines should be waived. Of course they were not, so vehicle owners routinely left angry threatening to sue the city.

City council meetings overflowed with law-abiding residents waiting for their one-minute turn to speak at the podium. They would demand that the city, and police force, take immediate action to eliminate the madness occurring in their neighborhoods. If not, they threatened to vote their elected officials out of office.

Politicians openly debated ideas on possible solutions to the problem, most of which were dumb at best. One of the craziest, or stupidest ideas ever heard was to have the city serve as a sponsor of weekly Sydeshow gatherings at the Oakland/Alameda County Coliseum with police monitoring the event. Of course, anyone with a reasonable amount of intelligence instantly recognized this idea was dumb because lawbreakers would definitely not agree to be monitored by five-o. Also, the A's baseball, Raiders football, and Golden State Warriors basketball teams would never agree to have their stadium parking lot ruined by tire skid marks.

***

Tonight's plan of misdirection for the police was to give them anonymous tips and social media information informing them that the Sydeshow would take place on Hegenberger Road. This location was right outside the Coliseum and featured a very large intersection leading to the airport with four lanes in each direction.

Hundreds of revelers arrived, saturating the parking lots of Denny's, McDonald's, Taco Bell, and other eateries in the vicinity, along with lining street curbs with their cars. Law enforcement officers flooded the area dressed in full riot gear with the sole purpose of keeping the peace. Unbeknownst to them, thousands had saturated Foothill Square and festivities were already out of control.

Montell Jordan's smash nineties' hit song, "This Is How We Do It," boomed from customized speakers inside the back of a Cadillac Escalade whose lift gate was open. The sound was so loud that it shook the ground and could be heard for blocks. Taco sat with his crew on the hood of his boy Catfish's ride, soaking in the scene. Having just been released from county jail a week earlier, he vowed to be more careful this time around and never go back.

Jakari "Taco" Nelson was bad news and a very dangerous individual. He was a miscreant. Feeling as if the world was out to get him, he trusted no one, except the small crew of outlaws with him tonight. A supremely gifted athlete with tons of natural talent, Taco was quick, fast, and strong. He stood six-three on a powerful two hundred and forty-pound frame and starred in all three major sports as a shortstop in baseball, quarterback in football, and point guard on the basketball court.

A handsome guy, Taco's skin complexion was what is known as high yellow. He had jet black hair, black eyeballs covered by dark brows, and a full grown mustache. A sinister sneer seemed like a permanent fixture on his full lips, and when he opened his mouth, you could not help but notice the shiny gold tooth he displayed with pride.

He was the neighborhood "coulda been" who felt as if the world was out to get him. Everyone agreed that he had the talent to become a professional athlete in any sport he chose but the reasons why it was not panning out were many. He "coulda been" drafted in baseball, but the coach didn't like him. In football, it was he "coulda been" given a college scholarship, but the coach played favorites and got mad when he refused to play receiver, so he made him sit the bench.

On the basketball court, he "coulda been" a high school All American, but his teammates were jealous because he was better than Lavelle Brookins. Of course. those theories were provided by his thuggish friends who both respected and admired him. On the flip side, former teammates like Bobby, D-Money, and Lavelle would contradict that by stating that Taco was self-centered, came to practices intoxicated or under the influence of marijuana, and refused to play team ball. Taco hated all of them and refused to even consider the fact that he was to blame for his own troubles.

> "Man, five-o really got fooled tonight." He laughed. "That text blast got these clowns here quick."

> "Honey, I'm hungry," said his girl, Synnetra.

> "Damn," Taco screamed. "I told you to get something to eat when we was over there with those squares on the basketball team, here." He handed her some money. "Bring me back a cheeseburger and fries."

> "Okay, Baby," Synnetra said as she made her way through the crowd.

Taco was angry that his girl waited until now to want something to eat, but glad in a way because he was hungry too. He couldn't stay mad even if he wanted to because she had stood by him throughout his nine-month incarceration. Every Saturday, rain or shine, she came to visit and always left money on his books for snacks. She was with him ride or die, no questions asked.

Synnetra "Nee Nee" Gant had been Taco's girlfriend for only a year, but to everyone around them, it seemed much longer. That was due in part to the chemistry between those two. From the very first time Taco laid eyes on her, he was infatuated with Nee Nee's strikingly beautiful features.

She was tall for a female, standing five-seven yet appeared much taller due to the high heels she always wore on her feet. With broad shoulders, her medium-sized softball shaped breasts stood proudly at attention without sag, accentuated by a small waist and flat stomach. Rather slender, Nee Nee possessed curvy hips with a nicely pronounced behind. Long legs, coupled with her hips and behind painted a beautiful portrait.

These attributes alone caused most dudes to drool on site but were not what blew Taco away. He was mesmerized by her facial features. A dark chocolate skin complexion was filled in with cat like oriental brown eyes, a long thin French looking nose, pouty lips like a Nigerian, usually coated by red lipstick, and a lean angular Brazilian jawbone and chin.

She changed her hairstyle weekly going from finger waves to a mushroom, press & curl, perm, weave, or puffy afro. The girl had a sassy look with the attitude to match and knew she looked good. She felt as though Taco was the perfect companion because he was not weak and, unlike most dudes she had known, would not let her run over him. He was the dominant force in their relationship and she had no problem with that arrangement.

Her family did not see it that way and were extremely disappointed by her choice of Taco as a boyfriend. They didn't care for him from the beginning because every time he came around he appeared to be intoxicated or loaded. This caused a severe rift between Nee Nee and her parents, especially her father who issued an ultimatum that she stop seeing him or move out. They were supremely surprised and hurt when she chose to move.

Taco, along with his boys, Catfish and Hot Link, drank liquor and smoked weed while casually taking in the stupidity going on all around them. With a smile coming from his sinister sneer, he scanned the crowd looking for Nee Nee. What he saw wiped the smile off his face instantly because Nee Nee was laughing as a dude hollered at her. This development did not sit well with Taco due to his jealous nature and immature insecurities.

"Aw hell naw," he screamed. "I know that negro ain't tryin to hollah at my broad," he said to his boys. "Let's go."

Taco, Catfish, and Hot Link headed through the massive crowd in the direction of Nee Nee and the dude who Taco thought was trying to make a play on his girl. The crowd was so massive that they were only moving a few feet at a time, yet Taco's eyes kept radar on Nee Nee, getting progressively angrier with each step he took. His boys, Hot Link and Catfish, followed with eager anticipation because those two hardly needed a reason to raise hell.

Elijah "Hot Link" Banks had been a hell-raiser all his life and brought nothing but misery to those who crossed his path. A master thief who also loved a good fist fight, Hot Link was even more dangerous with a gun. He would shoot you dead without provocation and think nothing of it. The reputation of a gangster, he gained within the city was far reaching due to his repeated trips to jail. A career thug, Hot Link was well known in criminal circles throughout the county.

His physical appearance did not scare anyone because he was only five-eight and barely weighed a buck fifty. Not one for fashion, Hot Link's normal attire consisted of baggy jeans and oversized wool shirt-jackets, however, underneath those clothes was a very powerful dude with muscles of steel from all the years of weightlifting.

Hot Link was blue-black, which is darker than midnight, and had several missing teeth. He wore his hair nappy afro style, using a sponge mitt to rough it up daily. His mustache and goatee were rarely trimmed and the scar running from his left ear down to the cheekbone was scary looking.

Unlike Hot Link, Catfish took great pride in being well groomed. Mustafa "Catfish" Rogers was a handsome, soft-spoken con artist. If Hot Link couldn't steal it, Catfish could definitely con you out of it. He stood six feet two with a bronze skin complexion, hazel eyes, soft wavy brown hair, and perfect sparkling white teeth. Catfish, just like Taco and Hot Link, was also powerfully built with the only difference being where Taco and Hot Link were more like pit bulls; Catfish was a Doberman.

Finally, the threesome approached Nee Nee, ready to battle as a young thug named Red was still trying unsuccessfully to get at her as she made her way through the crowd.

"Yeah, Baby," he said, "if you ever change your mind, I'll…"

Taco stepped in between Red and Nee Nee, speaking before Red could finish his sentence.

"Girl, what are you doing?" Taco demanded.

"Coming with our food, Baby, what's wrong?" Nee Nee asked.

"I see you talking to this negro. You think I'm stupid?" he screamed.

"Calm down, Baby," she reasoned. "That wasn't nothing."

"Nothing hell, you know I don't play" he yelled

"I know that" she yelled back "but I do think you're crazy, there's no need to be jealous, damn"

"Dude" Red said to Taco "the girl didn't do nothing wrong, you know, I tried to get at her and she told me she was with someone. Now seeing how insecure you are, I might as well go on and take her from you." he boasted to loud laughter from the crowd

"Homeboy," Taco pointed his finger at Red, "you need to step the hell off."

"Who's gonna make me?" Red challenged. "You?"

"I can, negro."

Sensing it was about to jump off, the crowd instantly formed a mini-circle with Taco and Red as the center attraction. Jelani "Red" Barnes was from the west side and backed down to no one. As if on cue, his boys faced off against Catfish and Hot Link with the circle expanding larger. Nee Nee tried to play referee.

> "Come on, Baby," she reasoned with Taco "let's go back to the car and enjoy the evening."
> "Yeah," Red cut in, "you better take that clown back to the car, Sweetness, with his no- game-having ass."
> "Look, fool." Taco was in Red's face now.
> "I done told you to step off."

Without warning, Red took a vicious swing towards Taco's face, grazing him on the cheekbone as he ducked before swinging back. Taco caught Red with a solid right hand that instantly bloodied his mouth as bets began taking place among the spectators on who would be victorious. Hot Link and Catfish, along with Red's two partner's, spread their arms wide keeping the crowd at bay as Nee Nee backed up, clutching the bag of food while biting down on her bottom lip.

Red attempted to throw another punch, but Taco ducked underneath, grabbing him around the waist before lifting him into the air and body slamming him violently on the concrete. Red was dazed from his head bouncing on the hard pavement and didn't realize Taco was savagely pummeling his face with left and rights until he was powerless to defend himself.

With Taco now serving a serious beat down, Red's boy made the mistake of reaching for his gun.

Hot Link saw it and with lightening quick speed, whipped out his own gun and fired. The bullet struck him in the center of his forehead killing him instantly. As his lifeless body crumpled to the ground in a heap, chaos ensued.

Upon hearing gunfire, the crowd scattered like roaches startled when the light comes on. Nee Nee screamed loudly while Taco casually checked his knuckles for cuts and bruises. Beat down and groggy, Red heard the shot, too, and attempted to get up and run. Hot Link kicked him back to the ground looking directly into his one eye that wasn't swollen shut.

"You should have stepped, negro," Hot Link stated.

Hot Link aimed the revolver at Red, smiling when he saw fear overcome Red's face. He fired shooting Red in the heart then turned and slowly walked away with the crew. Nee Nee shook like a leaf with Taco's arm around her for protection and comfort. From their casual demeanor, you never would have known they had just taken the lives of two young men who looked like them.

"What happened to that other negro, Fish?" Hot Link asked.

"Soon as you popped that first fool Link, dude got ghost," Catfish explained. "I didn't even see him."

Taco and Hot Link both looked at Catfish and roared with laughter as cars peeled rubber getting out of dodge.

3

FIVE-O

Only two hours earlier, Foothill Square had been saturated with thousands of revelers, spectators, and participants of the Sydeshow. To say it was a law enforcement nightmare would be the understatement of the year because to cops, especially those with military background, nothing short of the National Guard being called for assistance would derail that runaway locomotive.

The area now resembled a ghost town with the only people around leaving the bingo hall, getting gas at the service station, or purchasing booze from one of the three nearby liquor stores. There were small crowds of neighborhood residents idly standing by, waiting more to give police a piece of their mind than to provide information as to who murdered the two young black men lying on the ground covered with tarps.

Crime scene technicians had cordoned off the block with yellow caution tape and were busy collecting what little evidence they could find. Beat cops questioned members of the sparse crowd which consisted of residents, the homeless, dope fiends, alcoholics, and innocent passer-byes unsuccessfully. They could never understand how with thousands of potential witnesses, no one was willing to step forward with information on what actually happened.

Two coroner's staff employees leaned against the side of their department-issued vehicle, waiting patiently for an okay signal from cops to haul the bodies to the morgue. Once there, they would confirm the cause of death and provide police with positive identification of the victims. This was a crime scene that had gotten to the point of being routine where young blacks were killed, most likely by other young blacks, probably over something stupid.

Finally, a black Ford Explorer pulled into the parking lot with two burly homicide detectives in dark blue suits stepping out. One was black, the other white, and based on their demeanor, it was obvious to all they were in charge. One by one, officers approached in order to give reports on information gathered and witness statements.

Stepping off to the side in order to speak privately with the crime scene technician was Sergeant Norman Johnson. Coming from a long family history of cops, Johnson was known around the precinct as "Sarge," due to his take charge attitude. He stood six feet six inches on a solid two-hundred-and-eight-pound frame without an ounce of flab.

A former college football tight end, Sarge had served three tours of duty in Iran and was fanatical when it came to weight lifting. Clean shaven with a bald head, he had full lips and a large nose with flared nostrils. His eyes were a soft brown which complemented his milk chocolate skin complexion.

His father, Nathan Johnson, was a legend in the homicide unit and elated when his son decided to become a police officer. Due to retire at the end of the year, he was on cloud nine after his Norman passed the Sergeant's exam and received an assignment in the homicide division.

Sam Wang, the crime scene technician, walked over to Johnson with his trademark dead-panned facial expression. Just like Johnson, Sam was thirty years old with the only difference being he appeared no older than twenty-one. He stood five-seven and weighed in at one hundred and thirty pounds on a rail thin frame. He had jet black hair which he wore in a flat top with the sides faded style. His lips were thin, nose small, and eyes tight.

"What you got, Sam?" Johnson asked

"Not much, Sarge. Both victims were shot at point blank. One got it in the head and the other in the chest region. The shooter must have been either lucky or smart," Sam stated

"Why do you say that?" Johnson questioned.

"Because I couldn't even locate the shell casings from the weapon."

"Smart," Johnson replied. "He picked them up."

"Probably," Sam scratched his head.

"Anything else, Sam?"

"One of the victims took a terrible beating before he was shot so there is a chance I can find some DNA from the perpetrator, but it's a long shot at best."

"Well, it's better than nothing Sam," said Johnson

"Okay, Sarge, I'll let you know if something develops."

"Thanks, Buddy."

Sam walked away in the direction of the prone bodies with a look of determination on his face. He relished a challenge and considered a murder scene with no visible evidence the ultimate case. To Sam's way of thinking, criminals were stupid and always left a clue. Johnson's partner Lawrence Wratney walked over with a sour look on his face.

"What we got, Larry?" Johnson asked. "Not much, Norm," Wratney answered. "Two shooting victims, Jelani Barnes and Demaurio Gatling. Their driver's license list both with addresses on the Westside. Looks like Barnes took a beating before getting shot."

"Any witnesses?" Johnson asked, knowing the answer.

"Nope," Wratney answered dryly. "Seems everybody was preoccupied doing something else that caused them to miss the shooting. The rest claim to not have witnessed it at all."

"More like the stupid 'snitches get stitches' motto of the streets," Johnson said.

"Right," Wratney agreed, "Don't tell or you'll die, too."

"Until they kill one of your family members, then you want everybody to talk," Johnson responded.

As if on cue, a late model Chevy Malibu pulled up with a rough looking female jumping out running towards the dead bodies covered on the ground. Johnson and Wratney gave each other that knowing glance which meant, the family has arrived, as they made their way over to her. Word had reached Tasha Barnes that her brother, Red, was killed at the Sydeshow and she was determined to find out if it were true.

Tasha was openly gay and looked, dressed, and acted more like a man than a woman. She also fought like a man, having put a beat down on many men during her lifetime. Johnson and Wratney approached as she was struggling, nearly wrestling with officers to get around them. They continued to block her path, explaining to her that she could not contaminate the crime scene.

"I need to see if that's my brother," Tasha screamed.

"You'll have to wait until the crime scene has been cleared, Ma'am," an officer said.

"Can I help you?" Johnson asked.

"Yeah, I need to see if that's my brother," said Tasha, gasping for breath.

"And your brother's name would be?" Johnson inquired

"Jelani Barnes, but they call him Red," she answered.

"And your name is …?"

"My name is Tasha. Look, officer," she shouted. "Can we cut out the bullshit and let me go see if that's my brother?"

"Ma'am, you must realize I have to be certain that you are next of kin before allowing you to view the bodies," Johnson stated authoritatively.

"I have to be certain that you are next of kin," Tasha mimicked Johnson's use of proper language "Man, like I said--"

"That's Sergeant Johnson, not Man."

"I don't give a damn what yo' name is," she yelled. "I want to see if that's my brother."

33

"Okay, wait here," Johnson instructed.

Johnson and Wratney headed over to the dead figures covered with tarp and pulled them back, one at a time, looking at the bodies. After speaking in hushed tones, Johnson motioned for the beat cops to let Tasha come over for identification purposes.

Tasha stood with arms folded across her chest, tapping her right foot in an agitated manner. She wore saggy blue jeans, an oversized white sweatshirt, and blue and gold Warriors baseball cap turned around backwards. Several onlookers in the crowd were amused by Tasha's antics, but would not dare crack a smile for fear of reprisal from the thuggish-looking group of family members standing with her.

Finally, after what seemed like hours to Tasha when in actuality it was only minutes, Johnson motioned for to come view the bodies. She took one look then spread her arms wide with her head tilted back sobbing uncontrollably. She then began alternating from head back with arms outstretched to leaning forward to her waist while her hands covered her eyes.

"I know y'all seen it," she screamed at the crowd. "Somebody knows who did this," she hollered. "What you scared of?"

"So that is your brother?" Johnson asked.

"Yes, that's him" she answered, wiping away tears with her shirt. "And somebody knows who did it." She glared menacingly at the crowd.

"Can you identify the other one?" Johnson's tone was soft.

"That's Monk" she said solemnly.

"Monk?" Johnson questioned.

"His real name is Demaurio Gatling," she answered.

"Can you think of anyone who would do this?" Johnson continued.

"No, but I'll damn sure find out," she promised.

Johnson gave coroner's staff the okay to haul the bodies away then he and Wratney headed for their service vehicle. They would go to the precinct and write reports, review their notes, and wait for Barnes family members to arrive, demanding arrests be made and the case solved.

4

BAD ATTITUDE

Jeremy Haskins pulled into the assigned officer parking lot at police headquarters in road rage mode due to his two-hour commute from Oakley. He hated the daily ride which took him from his nice suburban home in East Contra Costa County to neighboring Alameda County and "The Jungle", which is what he called Oaktown. Usually, by the time he arrived for duty, he was ready to bust some heads and today would be no different.

Having never interacted with Blacks or Hispanics growing up, Jeremy was in dire need of diversity training. While it was a mandatory element of his job and courses were required, he did not pay attention in class and considered it a waste of time.

In the academy, all cadets had to address staff and the public with respect. During that nine-month training, Jeremy would grit his teeth and just barely whisper, "Good morning, Sir, or "Good morning, Ma'am," to African American or Hispanic custodial, gardening, or cafeteria staff of color. Once he became an officer, he would walk right past those same individuals without speaking.

He stood six foot one and weighed two hundred and fifteen pounds with a blond military cut, blue eyes, and thin lips. Throughout his six-year career, Haskins had numerous complaints filed against him for use of excessive force, yet never suffered disciplinary action. This was due in part to a strong union, which always seemed to get the charges dismissed as unsubstantiated and higher ranking officials slapping his wrist while writing it off as good police work.

The Police Administration Building, or P-A-B, as it was called, sat on the outskirts of downtown near the foot of Jack London Square. A massive concrete structure, the P-A-B covered an entire city block bordered by 6th, Broadway, 7th, and Washington. At the back of the building on 6th Street directly across from the precinct was the transportation lot which housed police vehicles and could be accessed from the building's basement by way of an underground tunnel.

Haskins always chose to use that entrance in order to avoid contact with people of other nationalities. As for cops on the force of different races, his interaction was minimal and only when absolutely necessary. Exiting his private car with the intent of taking the tunnel entrance to the building, he spotted his partner Bob Flaherty pulling into the lot for their scheduled swing shift assignment. Haskins lit a cigarette and waited as Flaherty parked and came over.

Robert "Bob" Flaherty was around the same height and weight as his partner, but the similarities ended there. He had jet black hair, a Chippendale model physique, and choirboy face clean shaven with a dynamic set of pearl white teeth. As Haskins watched him approach, he noticed Flaherty appeared to be deep in thought.

"Looks like something is troubling you, guy," Haskins spoke. "Had a rough night?"

"No," Flaherty answered "the night was fine. But there is something troubling me."

"Can I help? Maybe if you talk about it," Haskins responded.

"Maybe you can," Flaherty said, then continued. "I need to ask you something."

"Shoot," Haskins urged.

"Why do you do that?" Flaherty inquired.

"Do what?" Haskins asked a question of his own.

"Make up excuses to stop people."

"Make up excuses to stop people," Haskins repeated what he had just heard. "Listen, Bob, when you see a beat up car with three, four, or five young black hoodlums riding in it, ninety-nine out of a hundred times they are up to no good," Haskins justified it

"You know what you are doing is called racial profiling." Flaherty made his point.

"It's called being alert." Haskins justified his actions.

"I think you do it too much and have taken it to the extreme." Flaherty reasoned.

"Stop being paranoid Bob, one day you'll thank me for it."

Haskins flicked his still lit cigarette into the street before the two men walked through the tunnel into the basement of the P-A-B. Located in the basement were the locker rooms for male and female staff, an exercise room with a few stationary bikes, treadmills, and several weights benches with assorted weights of various sizes. There were also mirrors covering all four walls allowing one to view the activities of others while engaged in their own regimen.

The basement also housed the property unit in which citizens would claim property that had been stolen and recovered, taken away by cops and returned by court order, or to retrieve personal items that had been held during their jail time. The vice unit was also on that floor along with the firing range, which allowed cops the opportunity to sharpen up their shooting skills.

Scattered throughout the floor were tiny meeting rooms with most having only a small desk and two chairs. Right next to the tunnel was a large lineup room where officers reported for their daily briefing before hitting the streets. All of the areas in the basement were accessed by electronic key card entry except the cafeteria which was open to the general public and police staff.

Dressed in street clothes, which was the norm, Flaherty and Haskins headed for the locker room to change into their uniforms. Flaherty had only been on the force for a year and secretly hated being partnered up with Haskins due to their differing opinions on what police work should consist of. He found his partner to be overly aggressive, insensitive during interactions with the public, and rude.

Police officers filed into the lineup room for their swing shift briefing taking every available seat. Flaherty sat up front on the first row with a flip pad and pen in hand to jot down notes that could possibly be used during the course of his duties.

Haskins, which was his custom, hung around right outside the door until all seats were taken, then eased up to a back wall where he would stand with late comers or other malcontents like himself.

Standing at the podium up front was a captain named Oliver Frazier who reviewed his notes while everyone got settled in. The room was very noisy with discussions taking place amongst the cops, which ranged from details of arrests, dinner plans, dating, promotional aspirations, court appearances, and family issues just to name a few.

Frazier was a thirty-year vet, nearing retirement, and looked the part with bifocals propped on the bridge of his nose and thinning gray hair. He was short with a pot belly and wore a too tight uniform refusing to admit that due to lack of physical activity, his waistline had increased.

"Okay, listen up, Ladies and Gentlemen," Frazier addressed the room. "We know the sideshow will be jumping off tonight around midnight, but the location is still unknown. It seems like they send last minute text messages with fake locations in order to catch us off guard. We do have violence suppression units on standby in all three zones so when it jumps, we'll be there within minutes. We have also had a spike in convenience store robberies this week so be alert to that," he warned.

"In one of the holdups, the owner fought back, right?" Haskins shouted from the back of the room.

"Yes," Frazier answered. "He shot the suspect who incidentally was carrying a fake gun."

"That'll teach him a lesson," Haskins wisecracked.

"Or get the store owner killed," countered LaDarius Coleman.

LaDarius Coleman didn't really care for Haskins and the feeling was mutual. They had both graduated from the same academy where the bad feelings began. Coleman was a shade below six feet and built like a tank. He had a short afro, medium brown complexion, and full-sized nose and lips. He had a problem with Haskins attitude and superiority complex.

"Well, it nearly caused a riot," stated Frazier.

"Nearly caused a riot?" Coleman questioned.

"Yes, a riot," Frazier responded. "It appears that the suspect was shot in the back while running out of the store," he said before continuing. "Members of the community didn't take too kindly to that fact so they burned down the store. Our violence suppression unit had all they could handle in getting the owner away from the scene alive."

"Of course, it was okay for the suspect to be committing a crime right?" Haskins asked sarcastically.

"Why don't you just shut up, Haskins," Coleman shouted. "You can't just stereotype an entire community or race of people for the senselessness of a handful of knuckleheads."

"Here we go again," Haskins threw his hands up in the air. "Coleman to the rescue."

"Cut it out you two, enough of that," Frazier angrily stated. "Okay, listen up, on another issue. I have been receiving a tremendous amount of heat from upstairs regarding overtime. As I stated to you all before, we have been mandated to cut OT by fifty percent before the end of the fiscal year."

"With all due respect, Sir," Haskins was argumentative in his tone of voice. "Everyone knows we are short staffed by at least a hundred officers, so if you cut our overtime, who's going to protect the citizens? Oh, I got it." He snapped his fingers. "If they put some of those suits in upper management and internal affairs back in uniform, we wouldn't be short."

"Well, Haskins, from what I hear, they will be assigning some of the desk sergeants back to patrol and replace those positions with employees currently on workers comp."

"That's stupid," Haskins said. "We catch the crooks then hand them over to inexperienced beat cops to solve the crimes? Come on, man!" He raised his voice.

"Save your energy for another time, Haskins. I'm just the messenger. But I will say effective immediately you can no longer hang around with your suspects until investigators arrive."

"Then who is going to watch them if we can't?" Haskins asked.

"Look, Haskins." Frazier rose his voice. "Management knows that it's common practice to bring someone in near the end of your shift, then hang around for hours doing nothing until the detective's arrive."

"Do nothing?" Haskins shot back. "We're writing reports and hanging around as you call it, so we can give investigators first-hand knowledge of the case."

Grumbling could be heard throughout the lineup room as fellow officer's complained about this new mandate. Many of them had become accustomed to abusing overtime and considered the extra money as salary.

"Has our union been notified of this new rule?" Haskins inquired

"I don't know Haskins, but if they haven't, you can tell them. Okay, that's all for now, be safe out there" Frazier pointed to Haskins and Coleman "you two -my office"

Everyone walked out of the lineup room with many still complaining about the new overtime reduction rule. Frazier, Haskins, and Coleman marched down the hall and entered the Captain's office. Before the Captain closed the door Haskins spoke loudly to Coleman.

"Hey what's your problem?" he shouted.

"You're the problem," Coleman shouted back.

"Shut up the both of you, and sit down." Frazier slammed the door "Haskins, what is your issue?" he yelled.

"My issue is simple," Haskins said. "We average a murder every three days and seventy-seven percent of them are black on black, to which no one says a thing. Then when you have a store owner from Yemen protect himself and his business, the same black community wants to raise hell. What burns me up even more is when upstanding officers like LaDarius" he was sarcastic "try to defend this barbaric behavior."

"Coleman?" Frazier asked.

"I don't like it when Haskins throws the entire black race into his stereotypes. There are a lot of law-abiding, hard-working people in this community. Had he grown up anywhere like this, he would know it," Coleman retorted.

"Once again, I'm attacked for not growing up in the jungle," Haskins screamed.

"No, Haskins, just for your jungle mentality," Coleman stated calmly.

"Thinking like that will get you in trouble. Those are real people out there, many who are afraid for their own safety every single day."

"Okay, look, you guys." Frazier realized this was going nowhere. "I want you to keep your personal feelings to yourself and just do your jobs. Got it," he demanded.

"Yes, sir," Haskins said with a sly grin.

"Got it," Coleman answered.

"Good," Frazier stated. "Now get out there."

Coleman and Haskins walked out with each heading in opposite directions down the hallway. This wasn't the first time they had been called into the Captain's office and they both knew it would not be the last. Frazier sat at his desk for a few moments to regain his composure, then took the elevators for a ride to homicide located on the second floor. He hoped that group would take the overtime news better than the patrol cops had, but knew they wouldn't.

***

Captain Frazier entered the homicide office and frowned immediately. Of the eight investigators assigned to work swing shift, only four were present. The worked in teams of two which meant two teams had already left the building. Frazier knew that his impromptu meeting with Haskins and Coleman was the reason he did not have all of his detectives present.

Johnson and Wratney were typing up paperwork on their computers while Darnell Oliver and Socorro Gutierrez chatted silently in back of the room. Frazier grimaced in anger and gazed out the window, knowing he would have to repeat his spiel yet a third time due to the absent unit members. Motioning for Oliver and Gutierrez to join him up front, he sat down at an unoccupied desk.

Darnell Oliver walked over, grinning and shook the Captain's hand before sitting at his desk. Just like

Norman Johnson, Oliver had recently been promoted and was walking on a cloud. A superstar as a beat cop, his track record was impressive with him participating in, and initiating, many high-level drug busts. Growing up in the city, his name was mud to street hustlers and drug dealers alike. Even when he had nothing to do with their arrests, they still blamed him for snitching in order to get ahead and move up the ranks.

He stood six-one on a muscular two hundred-and ten-pound body, and always seemed to be happy, displaying a wide grin with an ear-to-ear smile. Possessing a gift for gab, Oliver was quick-witted and an analytical thinker. Everything had to make sense. His partner bounced up behind him and took her seat knowing just as the others what Frazier wanted to talk about. They had been briefed by the departing day shift unit.

Socorro "Coco" Gutierrez was a thirty-five-year old married mother of two sons. Her husband owned a successful plumbing business with eight employees, which allowed her the freedom to work swing shift. She has reddish brown hair, an almond skin complexion, beautiful hazel eyes, and full lips with sparkling white teeth. Her smile could light up a room and was always on display.

Strikingly beautiful, she stood five-seven with wide hips, a nice round behind, long chiseled legs and thighs, plus ample breasts and a flat stomach. Coco was often used as a decoy on prostitution sting operations to catch johns looking for a trick and was very good at it.

"Couple of issues," Frazier began, "we have to close some of these cases. The Chief and Mayor are all up my behind."

"Can't close 'em without help Captain," said Wratney.

"HELP! Whatever happened to good old-fashioned police work, Wratney?"

"Come on, Boss, you know what I mean. People see the murder, then nobody knows a thing. Without eyewitness's it's hard to solve a murder, much less prove it."

"Unless the perp is stupid and tells his girlfriend, who six months from now gets mad and spills every detail to us," Johnson added.

"Well, you need to figure out a way to get folks talking," Frazier stated.

"No can do, Sir," Johnson said.

"Enlighten me," said Frazier.

"It's ingrained from childhood and actually the police helped to make it that way."

"How so?" asked Frazier.

"Let me tell you a story." Johnson paused before continuing "when I was fourteen one of my friends father called the cops on some dudes who staked claim to their block and considered it their turf to sell dope. The police arrived and immediately knocked on my friend's door asking his father to verify that he had lodged the complaint. Needless to say, they were labeled as the neighborhood snitch family and began having their car tires slashed, bricks thrown through the front window of their house, and my friend became involved in quite a few fistfights for no reason. They had to move and never trusted the police again. I never heard from Rodney again, either." He stroked his chin

"Yeah, it was the same way in my neighborhood," Coco said. "When someone would get arrested, then an overzealous cop tells the person something like, '*That ain't what Jose said.*' Word gets to the street that Jose is a snitch then the next thing you know, Jose is dead"

"Any ideas on changing the cycle?" asked Frazier.

"The obvious answers are for teen girls to stop having all these kids, which results in babies making babies," Johnson said. "Then you need the man-boy's fathering these kids to stand up and be men, which is difficult because many never took the time to get an education and are unemployable. They are now angry at the world for being sorry and have no business fathering children. They just don't have the patience for it. But on the politically correct side my answer would be to start by trying to get inside the brains of the young kids, as early as five years old, let them know it is okay to be a police officer."

"Community policing will help bridge the gap because residents get up close and personal with their beat cop," said Wratney.

"We need the citizens to take back their communities, and the black churches to do more than just grandstand," added Johnson. "Oh, really." Frazier scratched his head. "Yes really" Johnson said "half of those nuts running around terrorizing the community have parents in church every Sunday praying for peace in the streets. These people know they can't even control their own house, much less when we show up they fall into that no snitch rule, out of fear" "Everybody knows what needs to be done," pitched in Wratney. "The problem is nobody's willing to do it." "Why not?" Frazier wanted to know. "Because the criminals will kill you and don't care about prison or dying, while the law- abiding citizen doesn't want to go to prison or the grave, so fear kicks in," Johnson told him. "I see. We need to figure out a way around that mindset," said Frazier. "On another issue which I'm sure you've all been made aware of. I've been informed by the Chief that we can no longer claim overtime from the time a homicide call comes in."

Darnell Oliver had been quiet throughout the entire discussion, simply listening as they talked about improving police relations within the community. However, when the subject became overtime, he sat up straight and jumped right in.

"So, when they wake me up at three in the morning I should roll back over and continue my sleep?" Oliver asked.

"Of course not," Frazier answered. "You just can't claim OT from three in the morning when the call comes in, then show up here at seven."

"What about when we go straight from our house to the crime scene?" asked Coco.

"That's another issue that I'm glad you brought up Gutierrez. They're also taking into consideration reducing the number of unmarked vehicles we use to get to and from work."

"Why would they do that?" asked Wratney.

"They say we are spending taxpayer money for our personal use by burning up free gas and reducing the life of city owned vehicles."

"What if we protest?" inquired Oliver.

"You'll probably wind up punching a time clock, Darnell," Frazier answered. "Look, I'm not the bad guy here, overtime for the department is costing the city roughly eight million annually and we collect three million alone out of that pot. I know they've been barking for years, but this time I have a feeling they have a little bite behind it."

"Okay, if that's the case, tell 'em not to call me in the middle of the night anymore until I speak to my union rep," Oliver said.

Just as he had done upon entering, Frazier grimaced, rose up, slowly glancing out the window, and walked out the door. He now felt like his retirement date couldn't come soon enough and secretly hoped would magically speed up. If it happened tomorrow, he had no problem with that.

5

<u>PAYBACK</u>

Mario "Blue" Barnes was on a mission to avenge the murder of his younger brother, Jelani "Red" Barnes, and after getting the news of Red's death along with the killing of his top lieutenant Monk, Blue was in a rage. He immediately learned that the third member of Red's crew, a low-level street hood named Day-Lo had been hiding out at his grandmother's house. Blue and his road dog, Scooty, considered Day-Lo a coward for running away and were hell bent on finding him to hear his excuse.

However, the task of tracking down Day-Lo would not be easy because he had vanished without a trace. At five o'clock in the morning on Sunday, they got the break they had been looking for as Blue got word that Day-Lo was at the Greyhound bus station on 20th and San Pablo waiting to catch a five-thirty bus to New Orleans.

Blue was ruggedly built in the mold of boxer Mike Tyson with a powerful upper body capable of knocking you out with a single punch. He had a mean streak and ran his section of Myrtle Street like a kingpin, where no one made a move without getting his approval before doing so.

 His partner in crime was Raphael "Scooty" Martin, a junior high dropout who only cared about drugs, drink, and women, not necessarily in that order. He was thirty-two years old going on fifteen with no purpose or sense of direction in his life.

Scooty was tall at six-four and very skinny like a number two pencil. Crusty black like a car tire in need of Armorall, he had a face covered with scratches and nature bumps. He also had big horse looking lips, buck teeth, and blood shot eyes from years of heavy drinking. Scooty was a follower and easily influenced by Blue.

They hopped into Scooty's black Ford Explorer and sped over to Greyhound, which was only three blocks from their rundown drug house on Myrtle Street. Blue had Scooty let him out the vehicle on the MLK side at the intersection of MLK and San Pablo which was only feet away from Day-Lo, but allowed the vehicle to be out of sight. Scooty's instructions were to wait exactly one minute then pull around the corner slowly.

***

Eddie "Day-Lo" Winston sat on the ground outside the Greyhound station covered by an old ragged blanket attempting to blend in with the homeless crowd until his bus arrived. He was nervous as all get up and felt that if he blended with the homeless, no one would recognize him.

His family tried to urge him to get there when the bus was boarding passengers, but Day-Lo refused stating he wanted to be on site in case the bus arrived early.

He had no idea that the moment he laid out among the homeless using his duffel bag stuffed with clothes as a pillow, he was spotted. A drunk named Cecil had just finished the last of his gin and was examining discarded cigarette butts tossed to the curb when he saw Day-Lo join the crowd.

Cecil promptly informed his drug supplier who relayed the message to Blue, and was rewarded a fifth of gin along with a gram of meth for his keen eye. Not wanting to share his goodies, Cecil went across the street to the Veteran's Administration employee parking lot and proceeded to get his groove on.

Day-Lo heard the attendant announce over the speaker system that his bus was now boarding and rose up from his spot to get on it. Suddenly and without warning, he felt himself being jerked off the ground as his right arm was pulled behind his back up to the left shoulder blade violently. Before he could move, an arm wrapped around his throat choking him so hard that he could not breathe. Next, he heard Blue's voice whisper in his ear.

"You make a sound, fool, and you're dead, now get in the ride," Blue demanded.

Scooty had eased up to the curb and already hopped out to open the back passenger door when Blue shoved Day-Lo's puny five-four, hundred-and-thirty-five-pound body head first across the seat into the other door panel. Jumping in right behind, he closed the door in one motion and began wailing away on Day-Lo's head and face savagely.

"Let my brother get killed and ran like a girl, huh fool?" Blue shouted between punches

"Blue, it wasn't like that man," Day-Lo pleaded through a bloody mouth.

"Then wouldn't answer my calls or text messages, huh, you coward."

Blue continued beating Day-Lo until Scooty pulled in the driveway of the drug house. By then he was groggy and punch drunk, failing to feel his cell phone vibrating. Blue tore the phone away from Day-Lo's pant pocket smashing it to the ground. He knew it was family calling in order to make sure that clown was safely on his way to Louisiana.

Grabbing a roll of duct tape from the back storage compartment, Blue snatched a piece off, tightly wrapping it around Day-Lo's head to cover his mouth. Together, he and Scooty drug Day-Lo to the garage where they would finish the interrogation. Throwing him unceremoniously to the floor, Blue began stomping his head into the cold slab of concrete.

"What happened?" Blue demanded, propping him onto a chair and ripping the tape off.

"I don't know, Blue, it happened too fast. They had guns, man. It wasn't my fault."

"Who did it?"

"I heard somebody call him Taco, please, Blue. I didn't do nothing wrong," he pleaded. "I couldn't hel…."

Before Day-Lo had a chance to finish the word help, Blue had plunged a knife deep inside his chest, killing him without a second thought. With assistance from Scooty, he put the body into the back storage compartment and drove to the football field at Mack High where they tossed it under the bleachers.

"Okay," Blue spoke to his partner. "We gon' get that fool, Taco."

"No doubt," agreed Scooty.

Driving back to the house, Blue placed multiple phone calls as Scooty did a poor job of cleaning up the blood stained garage. Within thirty minutes Blue had received information on Taco's normal hangout spots and a text message photo of Taco, lifted off Facebook. He decided to wait until nightfall before tracking down Taco.

***

The black Ford Explorer slowly cruised through neighborhoods on the city's eastside with the two occupants scanning the crowd intently at each location. They passed every location Taco was known to hang out at but continually came up empty. To them it didn't matter because they were out for revenge, and before the night was over, Taco would pay.

During the day, they had found out Taco rolled with a couple of hoods called Hot Link and Catfish, and that they drove around in an old school money green Chevy Impala with twenty-two inch tires and rims. Find the car, Blue was told, and you'll find Taco.

"Slow down, Scooty, you drivin too fast," Blue growled.

"What, you see somebody?" Scooty asked.

"Not yet, negro, but fast as you drivin I never will."

"Dude, those negro's probably sleep somewhere, you know they run around late night like us, it's too early" Scooty stated.

"Shut up, fool, they gone pay for what they did to my brother," Blue promised. "You just slow down."

First, Scooty had hit all the recreation center parking lots, including Rainbow, Arroyo, Carter, and Ira Jenkins. Then, he passed all of the parks – Sobrante, Willie Wilkins, Brookdale, Melrose, and San Antonio. Still with no luck, he began cruising through the liquor store circuit – 98th, 73rd, MacArthur, International, Seminary.

At a few of the locations, Blue would see a familiar face and get out of the car to idly chat with them. The conversation would be light-hearted before Blue acted as though he couldn't remember the name of the person who was soon to be his new drug connection. All he knew for sure was that dude drove a money green Impala with twenty-two's. Of course everyone he spoke with knew his real reason and played ignorant in knowing who he was talking about or where they could be found.

No one wanted to get caught up in that situation and be labeled a snitch for giving up Taco. Blue would have to find him on his own accord. As Scooty made his way down the list, he finally struck pay dirt at 25th and Foothill.

"That's the negro's car right there," he shouted. "Slow down, Scooty."

Hot Link and Catfish walked out of the liquor store carrying their booze when Blue opened fire from his rolled down passenger window, hitting them both. Taco, who was sitting in the back seat with another of their associates named T-Bone, instantly realized what was going on and returned fire wounding Blue. Scooty saw his partner take a bullet and sped away like a bat out of hell.

Taco and T-Bone jumped out of the car firing off several more rounds at them as Scooty put serious distance between them. Taco didn't care that stray bullets could harm and kill innocent people because his boys had been hit on a drive-by, so he was shooting back. After running over to check on Hot Link and Catfish, he and T-Bone returned to the car and sped away. They would definitely not be there to answer questions from five-o.

"I got hit. Take me to the hospital" Blue ordered.

"Don't die on me, Bro," Scooty screamed.

"Ain't nobody dying, negro. Take me to the damned hospital and drop me off."

"I'm going back to get whoever that was in the car," Scooty promised.

"Fool, don't be stupid, go hide my piece, then tell my Momma what happened."

Scooty drove eleven blocks to Highland General, which was the county hospital, and dropped Blue off in the parking lot of the emergency unit, then sped off. Blue limped inside the sliding glass doors, dripping blood everywhere before collapsing in the middle of the floor.

6

FAMILIAR SCENE

Several dozen onlookers watched out of curiosity as crime scene technicians cordoned off the area around the liquor store with yellow caution tape. Most had saw dead bodies before so watching police staff go through the process of protecting the crime scene from contamination was nothing new. They were more interested in seeing if Catfish would survive.

He lay stretched out on a gurney receiving treatment from paramedics for his gunshot wounds as coroner staff employees stood idly by waiting for the signal to do their job. One bullet had struck him in the leg, and the second wound, which was the more serious of the two, had come inches away from his heart. Medical staff knew they had to stop the bleeding for he had lost a massive amount of blood and if not treated soon at the trauma center, would probably die.

Within minutes after arriving, they rushed him to the hospital with lights flashing and sirens blaring. Hot Link's prone body lay motionless on the ground covered by a tarp as Sam Wang meticulously placed markers, which were small yellow cones, on top of the bullet cartridges for the purpose of bagging and labeling them as evidence.

Johnson and Wratney rolled up to the scene as the ambulance transporting Catfish to emergency flew right past them. Noticing the dead body covered by a tarp on the ground, Johnson went to question the store owner in hopes of catching the incident of security video. Wratney went in the direction of beat cops to get their reports gathered from witness statements. After speaking to the store owner, Johnson walked over to Wratney who was lifting the tarp off of Hot Link to inspect the body.

"Has this guy been identified?" Johnson inquired looking at the body.

"Elijah Banks" said Wratney "street name Hot Link, hangs out with the High Street Bank Boys whose group has been implicated in at least three murders within the last six months."

"Implicated?" Johnson arched his brow.

"The usual," said Wratney. "Rumors without facts, proof, or evidence to back them up."

"What about victim hauled away?"

"Eddie Rogers, better known as Catfish, also a member the Bank Boys. You get anything useful out of the store owner?"

"Maybe," said Johnson. "He said the shooters ambushed them, as soon as they walked outside. He also said there were two people in the back seat who returned fire on the suspect's car when the shooting began. He thinks they possibly hit one of the occupants. The suspects fled the scene in an older model Chevy Impala, green with twenty-two inch tires and rims."

"Do they have video footage?"

"Negative," Johnson answered, "the owner only tapes what goes on inside his business."

"Well, my report from first responders was that it was fifty-fifty on Rogers surviving. He lost a lot of blood," stated Wratney.

"We'd better head on over there in case he does survive," said Johnson.

The detective's waved at Sam Wang who was busy taking photos and drawing chalk outlines. They knew if he found anything of importance, they would be the first to know. When they reached the vehicle, a communications officer from central dispatch radioed them with information that a gunshot victim had just been admitted to Highland Hospital. Wratney activated the flashing lights without the siren, and burned rubber pulling off.

"Well, now," said Johnson, "the victim and suspect at the same location. How rare is that?"

"Maybe we should have bought a lottery ticket tonight, Norm." Wratney laughed

"Maybe we should buy one anyway."

Johnson laughed too.

The five-minute ride to emergency only took Wratney two as he had pedal to the metal all the way. Screeching to a halt in the parking area reserved for official vehicles only, the detectives got out and walked inside the sliding glass doors. During the ride, Johnson had asked dispatch to alert the hospital that they would be arriving shortly and to have someone ready to escort them to the security control room.

A nurse greeted them in the lobby and patiently waited while they spoke to the receptionist. She then led them through a maze of long hallways before stopping at a room next to a back stairwell. A burly looking Sheriff's Deputy met them at the door and took them to a monitor he had already cued up.

The room looked like an emergency operations center with huge eighty-inch flat screen monitors covering all four walls and giant fifty-five inch units situated in every corner. Three rows of tables housed multiple twenty-two-inch computer monitors recording all action both inside and outside of the hospital. Parking lots, stairwells, elevators, and even the bus stops surrounding the perimeter were monitored by security staff.

The detectives watched intently as Blue was being dropped off at emergency in a green Impala. A paper advertising sign had replaced the front license plate so they would not be able to identify the registered owner, nor could they make out the driver even after having the deputy zoom in from multiple angles.

"Hospital got a name for this guy?" Wratney asked Johnson

"Mario Barnes, street name Blue. His brother, Jelani, aka Red, is the victim from the sideshow killing Friday night."

"So this clown shot Hot Link and Catfish?" stated Wratney.

"I would agree," Johnson said. "Payback for his brother; only he got hit too. I'll request an officer be posted outside his room in case the perpetrator's come back."

"What about the entrance to emergency?"

"We'll post a few extra men out there and a patrol car in the parking lot. Let me go take care of that. See if you can get info from a doctor or locate some family members."

"I'll meet you back here," said Wratney. Johnson walked outside to their unmarked vehicle in order to speak with central dispatch. Wratney headed to the nurse's station with the hope of speaking to a doctor or directly to Catfish.

7

MAMA DRAMA

The waiting room at Highland Hospital was crowded, which was typical even for a Sunday night. Being the only trauma center in the county, they handled everything from shooting or stab victims to the uninsured. They also treated the mentally disturbed, cancer patients, stroke or heart attack sufferers, and those with cold or flu symptoms, along with many dealing with assorted aches and pains.

Sheriff Deputies were posted at the reception desk to keep people from showing out, which happened nightly. They also patrolled the hallways and guarded areas which were unauthorized for public use. Medical staff was kept busy throughout their shift by the constant flow of patients and worked hard for their money.

Most of those waiting had sour looks on their faces due to the long wait times it took to be treated. The more serious patients received priority, regardless of arrival time, so many who failed to understand that would become belligerent with nurse's or reception clerks. This often led to family members being arrested on the spot for acting a fool.

Martha Jones entered the reception area and waited in line for her turn to speak with the clerk. She wore tight fitting blue jeans which displayed a pretty nice figure, red high heeled shoes with a matching red blouse, and a flowing head of hair that was all weave. The longer Martha had to wait, the more rapidly her foot tapped, which caught the eyes of deputies who felt they should watch her more closely.

Finally, she went to the counter to speak with the clerk and after a brief conversation, was told to have a seat in the waiting room and a doctor would be out to talk with her later. Angry now, she marched into the waiting area searching for a place to sit. There was one seat available but the woman sitting next to it had her purse on the unoccupied chair and appeared to be saving it for a relative. Noticing Martha's eyes frantically scan the waiting room for a seat, the woman called her over.

> "Here, Honey, take this seat," she said while placing her purse in her lap. "My daughter's looking for a parking space so you know that will take hours." She laughed. "I'm LaDonna." She extended her hand.
>
> "Thank you. I'm Martha."

LaDonna Tittle wore a loose fitting white sun dress with red and green flowers as its design. Badly in need of a dentist, her teeth were brown from too much coffee and nicotine. She had a short afro, bulging eyes, and was blue black. Although she was skinny, she did possess large breasts and a round behind. Her appearance immediately screamed ghetto, welfare, and poor even to the casual observer.

Martha settled into the seat shaking her head in disgust at all the waiting patients and family members in the room. Her cell phone rang and she took the call engaging in a private yet loud conversation.

"They round here trying to kill all my kids" she said into the receiver "I got to move out of Oakland. Girl, I'll have to call you back, I need to find out what's going on with my son in surgery." She ended the call

"Honey, I wasn't ear hustling but couldn't help but hear you on the phone" said LaDonna "this is like the wild, wild, west out here. My son's in surgery too. I don't know what's wrong with these kids. They ain't got no home training, and be real disrespectful. I'm trying to move to Antioch.

"Girl, I know," said Martha. "My boys is some good kids, they just run with the wrong crowds, that's all. My oldest just got killed Friday night fooling around at that damned Sydeshow. They say he was just minding his own business when somebody walked up to him and shot him down like an animal. Now one day after we scraped up the money to have his funeral, my other baby been shot. He ain't even in the ground yet."

"That's terrible. I'm so sorry for you," said LaDonna.

"Thank you," responded Martha.

Wratney returned from the surgery unit without speaking to the doctor, who was still operating on Blue. The receptionist said something in his ear, then pointed to Martha sitting in the waiting room so he went over to question her. The moment he left, Tasha Barnes strolled in heading to the front of the line, looking wild eyed and ready to rumble.

69

Tagging along behind her was her girlfriend Domonique and another girl named Symone.

> "I want to know what's going on with my brother," Tasha hollered.
>
> "Ma'am, you'll have to wait your turn in line," said the clerk.
>
> "Wait in line. Hell, you're going to tell me something now," she demanded.

The deputy on guard rose from his stool ready for action. People in the waiting area heard the commotion and now ignored the television program on the wall monitor, instead focusing in on the Reality TV drama being played out by Tasha. Johnson reentered the reception area ignoring Tasha and her drama for he had more pressing matters requiring attention. Spotting his partner going into the waiting room, he followed.

> "Ma'am, he is still in surgery," said the clerk. "You'll have to lower your voice and have a seat in the waiting room."
>
> "What if I don't?" challenged Tasha.
>
> "You'll have to do as she said or leave," barked the deputy who was now flanked by two additional officers.

Tasha considered her options then turned and went to the waiting room. Wratney had just started questioning Martha when Johnson walked up joining them.

> "Excuse me, Miss Barnes?" Wratney asked
>
> "No," Martha answered. "My last name is Jones, but my son, Mario Barnes, is in surgery right now. How can I help you?" she asked a question of her own

"My name is Sergeant Wratney, OPD." He
flashed his badge. "I'd like to ask you a few
questions."

"I have a few questions to ask you first,"
Martha said.

"Okay, go ahead."

"Why hasn't anybody called me back about
my son who was killed Friday night at that
damn sydeshow?" She raised her voice.

The peanut gallery was now at full attention curious
to see what sort of drama would unfold. Scooty
walked up and stood behind Martha's chair.

"That would be Jelani?" Wratney stated
more as a fact than a question.

"Yes, Jelani, but everybody calls him Red,"
she answered.

"We're in the process of following up on
leads in that case. When we solve it, you
will be the first to know," he assured her.

"What I need now is to ask you a few
questions about your son, Mario."

Johnson cut in, directing a question at Scooty. True
to his nature, he had done something stupid by
letting Tasha and her home girls out at the
emergency entrance, then parking in a patient drop
off stall.

"Are you the owner of a Black Explorer
parked outside?" Johnson asked Scooty

"Yes, sir, is there a problem?" Scooty
inquired

"We saw you drop off Barnes at this hospital
on surveillance footage, now what we want

to know from you is what happened on Foothill and where is the gun he had?"

"I don't know what you're talking about," Scooty answered.

"How about if I took you downtown until you did know what I was talking about?"

"It's okay, Scooty," Martha said. "Tell them what you know."

"All I know is we were riding down Foothill, minding our own business when somebody started shooting. We got caught in the crossfire so I tried to speed away, but Blue got hit, then I drove him here and went to let Miss Martha know what was up," Scooty lied.

"And that's all you know?" Johnson pressed.

"Yes, sir."

"So you know nothing about the gun?"

"What gun?"

"Do you know the others who were shot?" Johnson asked.

"What others?" Scooty answered.

"Catfish and Hot Link," stated Wratney.

"Man, I told y'all we was just driving down the street." Scooty raised his voice.

"Okay, turn around." Johnson pulled out his handcuffs. "You're under arrest."

Johnson placed the handcuffs on Scooty's wrists and read him his Miranda Rights while LaDonna, who had sat quietly listening to the entire series of questions, rose up from her chair.

"Excuse me, officer, did you say her son was shot at the same place as my son?" asked LaDonna.

"And your son is?" Johnson asked.

"Eddie Rogers, the one y'all call Catfish."

"Wait a damn minute," shouted Martha who rose from her chair too. "You mean my son got shot by this Crackhead's son when all he was doing was driving down the streets?"

"Who are you calling a Crackhead, you stank Hoe," LaDonna shouted back.

The two women were standing face to face, so close that they could smell each other's breath. Without warning, LaDonna grabbed a hand full of Martha's weave pulling her head down while throwing several vicious uppercuts. Martha was scratching and clawing LaDonna's face in an effort to get free when Wratney attempted to separate the two women.

Johnson held Scooty by the handcuffs as mayhem ensued. Tasha and her posse began beating down LaDonna's daughter, then grappling with sheriff deputies who had rushed in to quell the disturbance. By the time the chaos ended, Martha stood holding LaDonna's dress, having pulled it off of her.

LaDonna stood in her underwear clutching a hand full of Martha's weave. The reception area had come alive with everyone being thoroughly entertained and the men foaming at the mouth over LaDonna's underwear clad body. She stood unfazed as both she and Martha struggled to get free from officers and finish what they had started.

"It ain't over, Ho," shouted LaDonna.

"Bring it on you, Dopefiend. We can take it outside right now," challenged Martha.

"Okay break it up before I arrest you both," threatened Wratney.

"Yeah, whatever," hollered LaDonna. "This ain't over," she promised Martha.

"Anywhere, anytime," Martha returned.

Johnson and Wratney hauled Scooty off to headquarters as deputies retrieved LaDonna's dress from Martha giving it back to her. First, they escorted Martha, Tasha, and their posse to Martha's car making sure they drove off. Fifteen minutes later, they repeated the drill with Ladonna and her daughter. The waiting area was now abuzz with chatter as people would be talking about the melee for the rest of the night. All of a sudden, their aches and pains were not as serious because as everyone knows, laughter is the best medicine.

8

THE DISCUSSION

Most students arrived for school suffering Monday morning blues, tired and sluggish from the weekend, which they felt went by way too fast. Word had already spread of the police stop to Lavelle Brookins and three other members of the basketball team on Friday night, so there was a mini buzz around campus. Lavelle, JP, Bobby, and D-Money gave vivid accounts of their encounter with five-o, fabricating the story to make it appear they put the cops in their place.

First period was a course titled 'Current Events" and being an elective, was considered easy to achieve a good grade. The class, wildly popular amongst students due to the dynamic instructor and lively discussions, was a "who's who" within the student body. Athletes and cheerleaders saturated the room with a few wanna-bees sprinkled in for good measure.

They enjoyed the opportunity to challenge jocks on issues other than sports to show that they were smarter in a neutral setting. The teacher sat at his desk reading a book while students filtered into the room taking their assigned seats. Once the bell rang, the teacher put his book down and stood up to address the class.

At the tender young age of twenty-nine, Thaddeus Tucker was a local boy who made good and returned to his roots in order to inspire others from the inner city to achieve their dreams. A former high school and college All American, his goal of becoming a professional basketball player washed out when he suffered a career-ending knee injury.

Having already completed the requirements for a bachelor's degree in economics, he earned his teaching credential and decided to use it in his old neighborhood. Thaddeus had a burning desire to empower young men and women, many of whom were facing the same obstacles and challenges he had to overcome growing up in Oaktown.

Those challenges included growing up in a one parent household, which usually was a mother with no male role model present. He also wanted to mentor young men on the consequences of doing the wrong thing, running afoul of the law by hanging with the wrong crowd, or winding up in jail or dead.

Not only popular with the students, as a single man, he was also adored by the female faculty who considered him a prize catch due to his good looks, charm, and outgoing personality. Addressed as "Coach T" by team members, they all took his class thinking it would be a breeze and he would let them slide by without doing the coursework. To their surprise, he required excellence from them and gave no free passes.

His team's success on the basketball court was received in the community with great pride, however, there was grumbling around the league from opposing coaches that he actively recruited players who should be attending other schools. A prime example, they claimed, was Jeff Peters.

Coach T ignored those gripes and subsequent investigations, which cleared him of any wrongdoings, with dignity and class.

He stood six-three on a chiseled two hundred and twenty-pound frame with hazel eyes and a peanut butter skin tone. With an average sized nose sitting above full lips and a short brown dreadlock hairstyle, he was considered handsome by all accounts.

A fashionable dresser, today he wore beige slacks with a matching belt, white button down shirt with brown stripes and open collar, brown penny loafers, and a light brown tweed sport coat that hung from the back of his chair. After taking attendance, he stood up, walked around the desk, and slowly began pacing back and forth across the floor.

"Good morning, class," he greeted.

"Good morning, Mister Tucker," they responded.

"Did you have a nice weekend?" he asked to groans from the students.

"Let's do something different today," he stated. "I want everybody to sit along the wall in a circle so we can all look at each other. If you would quietly move your desks, I would appreciate it."

Mister Tucker waited patiently while students noisily moved their desks and belongings. This gave students the opportunity to sit next to friends, or couples to sit by each other. Once everyone was in place, he stood in the center of the circle and continued.

"Okay, as you all know, our community is out of control due in large part to senseless shootings, which occur *almost* on a daily basis. Be it black-on-black or brown-on-brown, no one seems to have any clue on how to put an end to it. Generally speaking—and this is strictly my point of view," he paused for emphasis, "I think a lot of it has to do with the destructive attitudes of our youth in today's society. By that I mean getting shot for wearing the wrong color, be it red or blue. Or, being spotted in the wrong neighborhood such as Ghost Town, Sobrante Park, the Acorn, Seminary, 6-9 Village, Brookfield, and the list goes on. When you stop to think about it, those are really stupid reasons to take someone's life. Does anybody want to share their thoughts or opinions on that?" he asked.

The room was eerily quiet as students formulated thoughts into their brains. That was a touchy subject and many in class were afraid to voice an opinion for fear of having their point of view taken the wrong way or out of context. Mister Tucker knew they would be silent so he kept the pressure on.

"Let us talk about people getting killed because they live in an area code other than 5-1-0, like the 4-1-5 in San Francisco, or the 4-0-8 in San Jose, how about the 9-2-5 in Pittsburg. They come to visit a relative then wind up dead for the simple reason that they live somewhere else. And it goes even further than that with groups like the Nortenos versus the Surrenos, which pits Hispanics from Northern Cali against those in the southern part of the state, specifically Los Angeles"

They remained quiet but now he was ready to reel them in, and knowing how easy it was for Bobby to get irritated, he would get him going in order to spark the discussion. Bobby was not one to shy away from a verbal or physical confrontation and from serving as his basketball coach, Mister Tucker knew it.

"Today I would like to know your thoughts on why these senseless acts of violence occur so frequently. Bobby, I know you don't speak for all Hispanics…."

"He thinks he does," D-Money interrupted to laughter from the class.

"What are your thoughts, Bobby, on the causes and what can be done to remedy the situation?" Tucker asked.

"Well, Coach T," Bobby inhaled deeply, "everybody knows it's deeper than one simple solution. I mean some of these beefs go back generations like the Hatfield's & McCoy's in white history. You do have red against blue, Norteno against Sureno, but the bottom line is money. Everybody wants it and will kill you to get it. Actually, when you have a brown on brown murder it doesn't really get any press. It gets like a one paragraph notice in the paper."

"Why is that?" Coach T pressed.

"Because many of my people are here illegally anyway so they don't care about us killing each other" Bobby stated."

"So you believe most of the killings are due to the love of money?" Tucker pressed.

"Not only do I believe it," Bobby said. "I know it."

"Okay," Tucker responded. "Where does this money come from that they so easily kill for?"

"Drugs," Bobby answered emphatically.

"Of course, it's drugs," D-Money pitched in, "but they'll also kill you for looking at somebody the wrong way. It's the power of the pistol, I mean when someone's packing a piece, they feel invincible and ready to take on any and everybody. Without the piece, many of them are cowards."

"I agree," said Levitra who sat next to Bobby, "and it doesn't stop there. It's even here in the school and the main reason our senior numbers are so low."

"What evidence do you have to back up that claim, Miss Gant?" Tucker asked.

"We started with almost six hundred and fifty-nine people in the freshmen class," Levitra stated in a matter-of-fact manner, "and now we're down to what, three hundred and seventy-five seniors?" she continued without waiting for a response. "Maybe a hundred going to college and most a J.C. at that. I mean, I got girlfriends out there right now going for the dudes who got money."

"You have to understand, everybody's poor so it creates the haves versus the have-nots" Bobby said forcefully, "and either you got money, or you don't."

"So let me see if I got this straight," Tucker said. "You're telling me the senior numbers are low because everyone wants to sell drugs?" he questioned.

"No, that's not what I'm saying," Levitra shot back. "Some people have to work in order to help their families—they get pregnant—go to jail—get killed."

Levitra was now standing and with each statement slapped the back of her right hand into the palm of her left emphatically to get her point across. Most of her classmates nodded their heads in agreement while thinking about their own family situations. Coach T knew the subject was hitting her personally because her twin sister Synnetra had dropped out one week earlier to run around with his ex-ball player Jakari "Taco" Nelson.

Unlike her twin, Nee, who was measured in her words and spoke softly, Levitra, or "Vee" as she was called, had no problem letting the words fly. Just like her twin she stood five seven and always wore heels. She also possessed the same broad shoulders, softball-sized breasts standing at attention with no sag, a small waist, flat stomach, long legs, round behind, and exotic facial features. Coach T felt bad for Levitra because he knew the situation with Synnetra and Taco was causing her great pain.

"And that ain't all," Levitra continued. "Right here at school, you either buy your lunch or be on the meal plan, which we all know is high school welfare." The class erupted with laughter as Vee took her seat.

"You know, my friends call me a square for wanting an education and have a little jealousy that I'm getting a scholarship," Bobby said solemnly. "For most of them, this city is all they know."

"How can you call someone who doesn't want you to improve your life a friend, Bobby?" Tucker asked.

"Because sometimes they are the only friends I got," Bobby answered as the class grew silent again. "But if you want to talk about senseless murders, everybody ignores the elephant in the room." Bobby's voice rose dramatically.

"What would that be, Bobby?" Tucker asked.

"Black on *brown* crime, no one wants to talk about that." Bobby shrugged his shoulders.

"Black on brown crime," D-Money spoke. "Man, what you talking about?" he asked incredulously.

"I'm talking about blacks always kill or rob Mexicans, but it's never the other way around. We don't do that to y'all. Y'all rob my people selling ice cream or fruit from their carts and many are in so much shame because they can't speak the language that they go back to Mexico."

"Dude," D-Money's voice now rose, "your people commit just as many crimes against us as we do y'all. You break into our cars…"

"Wait a minute, you guys," Tucker interrupted. "We don't want to get into racial stereotypes; that's not the issue. Let's keep it on the subject at hand."

Bobby and D-Money both glared at each other with disgust. They had engaged in many disagreements over the years, but never one dealing with race, so for Bobby to make a bold statement such as that, it caught D-Money off guard. He now felt as though maybe he didn't know Bobby as well as he thought he did.

"Demonte?" Tucker asked. "Would you like to elaborate on still calling people friends who are jealous of you?"

"Yes, Sir," D-Money said. "Sometimes your friends are all you have and this city is all they know. I mean, so many of our friends have never been to Fisherman's Wharf and its only fifteen minutes away. All they know is the craziness that goes on in these streets."

"Okay," Tucker stated. "Let us change subjects right here, but I would like you all to come prepared tomorrow with solutions to the problems we just covered. That's your homework assignment. Now, let's discuss another subject that is all over the news today and has become a sticky issue in race relations."

"After this, what else is left to discuss?" Levitra questioned.

"Glad you asked, Miss Gant," he said. "The number one dilemma facing our country today is the issue of cops murdering young black men for no apparent reason, and in many instances, getting away with it. To most black people it's nothing new. Only now with the explosion of social media and cell phone videos it has come to light."

Suddenly, Tucker's eyes looked toward the door and a smile formed on his lips. Standing there motioning for him to come outside was a beautiful teacher named Diana Meadows who taught English in a class next door to his.

"Okay, class, excuse me for a moment. Gather your thoughts for the discussion so that when I return, you'll have something to contribute."

With that said, Tucker bounced from the room leaving the students alone. The school grapevine had those two as an item, yet no one knew for sure. They did all they could to keep appearances on a professional level, but there were signs, such as this interruption, that something was going on.

All of the students were in agreement that if Coach T was going to fool around with any of the teachers at school, Miss Meadows would, or should be the one. She was right around his same age and had also been a standout college athlete. Just like Tucker, she was extremely popular with students and as both the cheerleader and girl basketball coach, her after school activities kept her in close proximity to him.

Diana Meadows stood six feet one and had been a high school All American in both basketball and volleyball. Choosing volleyball as her sport in college, she excelled and was invited to the Olympic trials as a junior, to which she declined due to nagging injuries. Her lifelong dream was to be a school teacher and after earning her teaching credential, she fulfilled it.

Diana had aqua blue eyes covered by unflattering bifocals, a long pointed nose, and medium sized lips. Her blond hair was usually wrapped in a bun and she dressed conservatively in business suits. For cheerleading and basketball practices, her normal attire was loose fitting sweat pants and oversized sweatshirts. For all of her life, Diana had been a tomboy at heart, but now a change was evolving.

Not coincidentally, that change coincided with the arrival of Thaddeus Tucker to the school. First, she began turning heads after school in the gym where she would arrive for practice wearing hip hugging shorts favored by volleyball players which accentuated her massive legs and thighs. She also wore athletic bras beneath form fitting tank tops displaying a six pack midsection and mouth-watering breasts.

Fellow teachers also noticed her change in appearance as she came to school decked out in hip hugging skirts barely covering her creamy thighs, along with allowing her hair to flow freely. The jealousies started when she covered her lips with gloss which gave them a juicy delicious sheen and the bifocals came off. Diana's was a hidden beauty that was only revealed when she met Thaddeus Tucker.

The moment the door closed, many of the students whipped out their cell phones in order to visit various social media sites. Although Facebook was the world's most popular site, the teens in class considered it old and out of style. They now preferred Snapchat because it allowed them to record and post videos which would automatically erase themselves after twenty-four hours. They also used Instagram to post photos or Kik, which most of their younger siblings used to text message each other. D-Money was having none of it, for he had an issue with Bobby to settle.

"So, Bobby," D-Money spoke. "Why do you want to say blacks rob and kill Mexicans?"
"Because it's the truth, Dee, plain and simple," Bobby answered. "They robbed my mother's cousin yesterday while he was selling ice cream from his street cart. Just walked up and went inside his pockets, taking his money. Since it was four of them and he couldn't speak the language, he let them out of fear."

"I'm sorry for your cousin, Man," D-Money responded truthfully, "but that doesn't make us all bad. Look Bro, all races have bad seeds, not just blacks."

"I know, man, my bad, it just pissed me off that's all," Bobby apologized.

"Okay, you girls, give each other a hug," Lavelle said to a loud laugh from the class.

Bobby and D-Money rose up and hugged each other as Mister Tucker was entering the room. Upon seeing the two embrace, he smiled and returned to center circle.

"Okay," he readdressed the class, "as I was saying, young men of color being killed by police has become a hot button issue around the country. Many protest groups have sprouted up to challenge officer involved shootings with the most notable being the Black Lives Matter movement. Those of us living in the inner city know it has been going on for decades and has only come to light because people are now able to video record the incidents on their cell phones, then post it immediately on social media. There are too many instances to name them all, but I'll start with a few that have taken place here in our city." He paused for a moment to collect his thoughts.

- "Alan Blueford – After being chased a few blocks by police, he tripped and fell. Officers said he pointed a gun at them while on the ground and fired off four rounds, three struck him with the fourth hitting an officer in the foot. The coroner's report found no gunpowder residue on his hands—no drugs or alcohol in his system."
- "Oscar Grant was killed by a white transit cop while being held on the ground."
- "Franswa Raynor – allegedly robbed a restaurant employee. Officers said he made a move to his waistband and shot him in the face. He was treated at a hospital and arrested. The next day he was released and no charges ever filed."
- "Demouria Hogg – fire department personnel found him unresponsive in a car and called police saying they saw a handgun on the seat. Police

shattered the passenger side window with a metal pipe awaking him. One tased him while another shot him dead saying a confrontation occurred."

The room was silent as Mister Tucker spoke with most students, either taking notes, doodling, or listening intently.

"Anyone have thoughts, comments, or opinions on that?" Mister Tucker asked as the room remained silent. "All right," he continued.

- "On a national level, Michael Brown – killed by a white police officer in Ferguson, Missouri."
- "Philando Castile was killed by a white cop during a traffic stop in Saint Anthony, Minnesota."
- "Alton Sterling was fatally shot by two white Baton Rouge, Louisiana police officers while being held on the ground."
- "William Chapman was shot in the face and chest outside a Wal-Mart store in Sherman Park, Milwaukee after a security guard accused him of shoplifting. There was no video recording of the shooting, and testimony conflicted on the details. In this instance, that officer, one Stephen Rankin was fired. These

shootings and other have sparked a nationwide outrage not only by blacks."

"Can I say something Coach?" D-Money cut in.

"By all means, Demonte." Mister Tucker spread his arms in a sweeping motion across the room "the floor is all yours" he sat down as D-Money stood up.

"I mean not to defend police, but in most of those cases you named, black men were breaking the law. It seems to me like they should have Black Lives Matter when we kill each other. You had two people shot at the Sydeshow Friday night with hundreds of folks there, yet nobody stepped up to say they saw it."

Before D-Money could sit down, Venitra shot out of her seat like a cannon.

"How dare you say that, Demonte?" she screamed. "You should be ashamed to call yourself a black man. Our brothers are out there killing each other because the system is set up that way. They can't get no jobs, locked in prison all their life for petty crimes, have to work twice as hard just to get half as much as whites do" she was once again slapping her right backhand into her left palm "I don't care what they were doing, that doesn't give the police the right to kill them. It could be your brother, cousin, father, uncle, or even your son if you ever have one. I'm ashamed of you." Levitra went to a seat on the other side of the room, glaring menacingly at D-Money as she sat down.

"See that's what I mean," Demonte said.

"Okay," Mister Tucker cut in. "Jeff, you've been quiet."

"The way I see it," JP said, "is All Lives Matter. Cops killing blacks, blacks killing cops, it's all wrong but that doesn't give you the right to blame it on whites Venitra, or say stuff like you have to work twice as hard to get half as much as we do."

Venitra stood up, but Mister Tucker motioned for her to sit down, so JP continued.

"You need to check your history when you begin talking about the past because if you did, you would know that slavery began with blacks selling other blacks to the white man for money."

"Wait a minute, JP." Lavelle finally spoke up "how could blacks sell blacks to the white man when they spoke different languages?"

"Check your history, Lavelle," JP responded. "It's a fact."

"Is that what they tell you in the suburbs?" Octavia asked as if she couldn't believe what she had heard

"No stereotyping, Miss Wilson," Tucker admonished.

Octavia Wilson had the build of a track star, which she just so happened to be. With a skin complexion as yellow as buttered popcorn, she favored bright red lipstick painted on delicious mouth-watering lips. Sporting a gold dyed short curly afro, she was blessed with curves in all the right places. The girl was super fine.

"Oh, my bad, Mister Tucker," she said. "What you have to understand, Jeffrey, is that whites steal everything we have."

"What have they stole?" He didn't know where she was headed with that statement.

"They steal our lips, they steal our butts, they steal our music, they steal our dance, they want our men and the men want our women. Then to top it off, they feel threatened by us so they resort to stereotyping our brothers, fathers, cousins, uncles, and sons as lazy and dangerous. Of course, you wouldn't understand because you have what is known as white privilege." she snapped her finger and swiveled her head.

"White privilege," JP reasoned. "I'm not privy to anything."

"Privy" she mocked "you don't get followed around in stores simply for being white. You don't get the maximum sentence for doing the minimum crime, passed over for jobs when you're the most qualified candidate, denied promotions or raises, have people go to the other side of the street because they see you coming towards them ..."

"That has nothing to do with what we're talking about, Octavia, and you know it." JP interrupted her sermon.

- "Gavin Long, black, of Kansas City ambushed white cops in Louisiana."
- "Micah Xavier Johnson, black, ambushed cops in Texas."
- "Lovelle Mixon, black, ambushed cops right here in this city."

91

"So what you're telling me is that those murders were justified?" he questioned.

"Dude, you don't get it," she said.

"Okay, everyone." Mister Tucker spoke. "For the remainder of class we will break off into groups of four to discuss these issues. I need one person in each group to record the ideas and statements made. I would also like you to select a spokesperson for your group."

The class was now alive with sidebar conversations going on throughout the room. Many who entered as friends would now leave as foes. Mad at each other because they didn't agree on the issues discussed. Venitra had no idea Demonte felt as he did, but knew she could no longer date him. Bobby was mad at the world and Lavelle considered reevaluating his friendship with JP.

When the bell rang for class to be dismissed, the groups were still engaged in highly charged conversations and had not come close to presenting their findings to the others.

"Okay, everyone." Mister Tucker spoke as they shuffled out. "We will finish this up tomorrow. Please come prepared." He began straightening up the room.

"Hey, Vee," Lavelle called Venitra.

"What's up Lavelle?" she smiled.

"Saw your sister the other night" he said.

"Running around with Taco?" she asked.

"Yep, what is she doing?" he asked a question of his own.

"Screwing up her life. Hope she don't get pregnant by that fool." she gritted her teeth.

"Must be tough on your parents, huh?"

"It's killing my Mom" she answered. "Daddy is trying to play the tough love game, but I know he's hurting."

"I hope Nee gets it together," Lavelle said.

"I do, too," Levitra stated.

"Baby, let's go get burritos for lunch," D-Money said to Vee.

"Not today" she told him "I'm having lunch with the girls."

Levitra walked away with Octavia and their crew as Demonte stood there looking stupid. It was only then that he realized he would have some explaining to do. JP walked out the class wondering where Lavelle had gone. They had the same second period English class and always went there together. The friction developed was something none of them had experienced before.

9

PARTNERS

Haskins pulled into the lot at the P-A-B for his Monday swing shift assignment. Parking in the first vacant stall he could find, he got out, immediately firing up a smoke. As usual, he was in a sour mood from the commute, but today he was upset because of other issues also. Noticing his partner's car already parked, he headed for the building.

Due to the Sydeshow becoming top priority on Friday and Saturday nights, all available staff was required to be on duty. This meant Haskins had to work every Saturday, which was his normal off day. Most of his fellow officers had no problem raking in the overtime, but to Haskins, he shouldn't have to work OT on a mandatory basis.

He had worked six days a week for over a month and did not like it one bit. His second issue was with LaDarius Coleman whom he felt defended Blacks no matter what sort of hideous crime they would commit. Haskins hated Coleman and felt that sooner or later, things would come to a head and they would resolve their differences, man to man.

The most troubling issue on his mind, however, was his partner, Bob Flaherty. He had spent his entire Sunday off day drinking beer while replaying his parking lot conversation with Bob. The words Flaherty spoke were still ringing in his ear.

"You know what you are doing is called racial profiling," he recalled Flaherty saying.

That statement had left Haskins steaming and ruined his day off. He now felt as though he could not trust his partner because they were not on the same page. After changing clothes in the locker room, he went to the lineup and did his regular routine of hanging around outside the door until all seats were taken.

Assuming his spot on the back wall, Haskins was unusually quiet throughout Captain Frazier's briefing. The silence caused several of his back wall cronies to ask him if anything was wrong. It was out of character for Haskins to be quiet and not comment negatively on multiple issues addressed by Frazier.

Flaherty also noticed Haskin's silence but was not surprised. Their entire Saturday night shift had been tension- filled due to their parking lot conversation. It was so thick you could cut it with a knife. Based on the way Haskins was acting, Flaherty knew tonight would be more of the same. Just like Haskins, he had spent his entire Sunday thinking about their issue, minus the beer.

He'd also weighed the pros and cons of transferring to the Eastmont precinct to get away from Haskins, not caring if that meant working a different shift. To continue riding with Haskins would sooner or later certainly present a problem, or so he reasoned. After Frazier dismissed the group, Flaherty headed for their patrol car while Haskins seemed to disappear. Two minutes later, Haskins got inside complaining as they drove off.

"I don't like that guy, always trying to stick up for criminals. Talking that crap about me stereotyping an entire community," Haskins barked.

"Well, he's not that far off, partner," Flaherty countered. "You do tend to go to the extreme sometimes."

"Oh, so now you're on his side?"

"I'm not on anyone's side, just saying that sometimes you are a little high strung"

"High strung" Haskins screamed "hell we're dealing with freaking animal's man, every freaking day"

"Jeremy" Flaherty's voice rose "If I were in Coleman's shoes, I could see myself viewing you as a racist."

"What kind of proof do you have for a statement like that?"

"From the references you make about people of color" Flaherty said "Coon eyes, Baboon, Porch Monkeys, Wetbacks, Moon Face, you talk bad about every race except your own"

"You sound like you want a new partner Bob?"

I've been thinking about it" Flaherty answered truthfully

"Screw you" Haskins shouted

Now that each man had put their feelings out in the open, the silence was deafening. Haskins would answer radio calls from central dispatch while Flaherty drove to the locations. On their dinner break, Flaherty went inside the restaurant and sat down to dine while Haskins ate in the car. Darkness fell upon the city with the men still ignoring each other when a call came in from central dispatch.

"All units, two-eleven in progress at a convenience mart, address 2701 Foothill."

"Unit twelve on the way. Estimated time of arrival - one minute," said Haskins.

"Suspect is described as African American, six foot two, one hundred and seventy pounds wearing blue jeans, dark colored hoodie, and white tennis shoes - consider him armed and dangerous," warned the operator.

"Ten-four," responded Haskins.

Flaherty activated the lights and siren, which was called a code two, then mashed the accelerator, burning rubber. The convenience store robber had struck again but this time, Haskins felt, would be his last.

10

THE HOLDUP

Jalen "Spunk" Vance had been on a meth-fueled high for the past three days and had spent all the money taken from his last convenience store holdup. Spunk knew he needed money fast or his drug induced high would come crashing down in a hurry. Before he could let that happen, he would have to rob again.

Once upon a time a successful musician and songwriter, Spunk's drug and alcohol usage ruined what should have been a promising career. Having performed at all the local nightclubs and on the church circuit, his story was well-known in the community, however, this was not the first, or last time it would repeat itself. The names and faces may have changed but the end result was always the same where a truly gifted artist had let it all slip away in a very short amount of time.

Spunk's instrument of choice was the keyboard, but he could also play drums, bass guitar, and sing. His problems began a year earlier when he attended an after party following a gig. Drugs were flowing plentiful which was nothing out of the ordinary, however, a female companion encouraged him to hit a joint of weed laced with meth.

Normally, Spunk refused anything other than weed and a little drink, but on that particular night he allowed himself to be convinced by the woman to try it one time. That was all it took as the euphoric rush to his brain from the first hit had him hooked. After that, Spunk always seemed to have a meth laced joint in his mouth. He eventually graduated to injecting it because smoking did not give him the same instant gratification as it once had.

Then he began selling off his collection of musical items, missing rehearsals and gigs, and borrowing money without paying it back. Once the explosive temper tantrums and change in mood swings rose up their ugly heads, other musicians stopped fooling with Spunk. They didn't care how talented he was; it just was not worth the trouble.

Without the cash flow coming from gigs or playing in church, Spunk resorted to stealing from family and friends. He would not steal from strangers for fear of getting caught and hurt badly, but family was fair game. The little bit he did manage to clip off of relatives was nowhere close to what he needed to supply a now raging habit. He had a monkey on his back that he had to carry so he chose to rob convenience stores.

Spunk felt like convenience stores were easy targets because since they stayed open twenty-four seven, he could hit them late at night when only one person was on duty. Lately, however, he had been robbing them as soon as the sun went down. Tonight, he would hit Quik Stop on 27th & Foothill because since they were always busy, there was bound to be plenty of cash in the registers.

There was also heavy foot traffic in the area with dealers, users, and thugs saturating the area as if it were downtown at high noon. He felt that once he held up the store, it would be easy to blend in with the crowd during his getaway. Quik Stop sat on the corner with a triangle shaped parking allowing entrance from Foothill or East 17th Street.

At the edge of the lot was a taco truck, which seemed to always have a line of customers waiting to buy tacos, burritos, quesadillas, or torta sandwiches. The truck got its electricity from a pole displaying the stores neon sign, to which they paid the store owner a large monthly usage fee.

The area was dominated by blacks and Hispanics living in massive housing complexes with most of them old and in desperate need of repair. Illegal activity was the order of business and the streets were alive twenty-four seven. Spunk drove a beat up thirty-year old Honda Civic, which had seen its better days.

Riding down Foothill, he drove past the store then turned right on 26th Avenue one block over. Parked in the first available spot on the street, he got out heading for his mission. There was a bus stop right in front of the store with many people waiting so Spunk lingered amongst the crowd as if he was waiting too.

Watching store activity like a hawk, Spunk waited until the coast was clear and no customers were inside then made his move. Putting on a pair of dark sunglasses and pulling a hoodie over his head, he pulled out his weapon and rushed inside.

"Give me the money," he demanded. "Make one move for a gun or the silent alarm and you're dead."

The cashier, who was alone, began sweating profusely and trembling at the sight of Spunk's gun aimed at him.

"Please don't shoot," he pleaded. "I give you all the money."

"Hurry up, fool," shouted Spunk. "All of it."

The cashier was just about to place the larger hundreds and fifties into tubes which would be inserted into a slot and automatically deposited in the safe when Spunk walked in on him. Handing over the giant wad, he cleaned out the register of smaller bills and gave them to Spunk watching as he stuffed the money into his pocket.

Running out of the store, Spunk hit the wind hightailing it to his car. There were so many people outside that he had to zigzag through the crowd. Unknown to him, one of the customers in line at the taco truck witnessed the robbery and called police. Spunk was surprised to hear a police siren in the distance so soon after the heist getting louder by the seconds.

Hitting the corner of 26[th,] he nearly ran over a guy heading in the direction of Foothill. Deftly avoiding the collision, he jumped into his bucket and sped off. After a few blocks, he no longer heard the sirens so he slowed down and went to pay a visit to the dope man.

11

MAKE UP

Levitra lay sprawled out across the bed in her room, talking on the phone with Octavia. They were discussing the current events class in general, and Demonte and Jeffrey in particular. She was still furious that her dude had the nerve to say what he did about black people in an open forum and wondered if he truly believed it. Octavia was angry at JP for having the nerve to defend the police and his own race for doing blacks wrong

Vee's parents were gone to their weekly bowling league matches in nearby Alameda leaving her home alone. The house was situated on 26th Avenue, a rather quiet block, considering the neighborhood, between Foothill and East 17th Street. Painted white with green trim, it was built in the 1940's and had three bedrooms, one bath, and neatly manicured front and back yards. It was the only home Vee or her twin Nee Nee had ever known and with both parents living there, they felt safe and secure. Her mother Lenora worked for the post office as a mail handler while her father George was employed by the school district as a head custodian. The Gant's were upstanding citizens and took pride in raising their daughters the right way.

Deciding to get a snack, Vee ended the call with Octavia and wandered into the kitchen when the front doorbell rang. She knew who it was but did not go to answer it. After a few more chimes went unanswered her cell phone began ringing to which she ignored that too. A couple of minutes later she opened the door to find D-Money sitting on the front steps.

  "I knew you were in there" he said. smiling.

  "Demonte what do you want?"

  "Don't tell me you're still mad because of today."

  "You don't even want to go there, mister Boise State." She was sarcastic.

  "Can I come in?"

  "Boy, you know my parents don't allow dudes in the house when they're not home."

  "Vee, what are you talking about? I've been in here many times when they were gone and you know it! You need to stop tripping and let's talk about it."

  "I don't have anything to say to you and the only reason I let you in when they were gone is because my sister was here. After what you said today, I'm not sure if I trust you anyway. As a matter of fact, I don't even know you."

  "Girl you need to quit tripping and let me explain" he said.

  "Explain what, Demonte?" She was loud.

  "Listen, I wasn't defending the police. Of course they're wrong for killing unarmed black men in cold blood. All I was saying was that the same energy our people have when a cop kills an unarmed black man is the energy they need to have when a black kills another black. When that happens you don't see Black Lives Matter marching and protesting. Why not, Levitra?" he asked. "I'll tell you why." He answered before she could respond. "Because there is no glamour in that, plus, they would have to identify the suspects, which could put them on front street and have them labeled a snitch. See, they'll tell on police because they know the cops are not coming into the neighborhood to find them for snitching. It's a whole different ballgame with hoodlums though, because they'll get you, so when I say what I say, I say it because of that, if that makes any sense to you."

She stood there thinking about what he said before responding.

"You said they were all breaking the law before being killed...."

"I didn't say nothing about before being killed," he cut in, "but most of those dudes were breaking the law," he stated.

"That still doesn't give the police the right to kill them when they are unarmed, and all of them were *not* breaking the law," she debated.

"See, you're twisting my words. I said *most* of them."

"Shut up, Demonte. Matter of fact, what do you want, Boy?"

"I would like to come in." He smiled again.

D-Money possessed a smile so warm that it could melt ice and Levitra, no matter how upset, could never stay angry at him for long. She knew he had a kind heart and deep down knew what he meant about black on black crime. They had been each other's first love, a couple for nearly five years, and were considered a unit by everyone within their inner circle.

"Don't be giving me that look either." She softened.

"What look?" He stood up, facing her still smiling.

"I know what you're trying to do but it's not going to work."

"What are you talking about?"

D-Money kissed Vee passionately and she returned the kiss with an equal amount of passion to him.

"Okay, come in, boy," she relented.

The teens sat on the living room sofa kissing and holding each other for the next thirty minutes before Vee opened up her school books to finish up homework she had been working on earlier.

"I still don't understand why you have to go so far away to college," she stated.

"Honey I have to go where the scholarship is at, I'm not an all-american so I don't get to choose Kentucky, Louisville, the Pac 12 – none of them. But I do plan on putting Boise State on the basketball map *and* making the NBA."

"You need to plan on getting that degree in case the NBA is not an option" she warned.

"You know I make good grades," he boasted.

"I know," she kissed him. "Just don't be making straight *A's* with the women, mister basketball star."

"That ain't the problem," he said.

"What's the problem, Mister Edwards?"

"The problem is you keeping those dudes in check around here."

"Get out of here." She laughed. "You know I don't want nobody else." They kissed again.

"I have to go before I miss my bus, if I leave now I can just make it."

"Can't you take the next one?" she asked.

"I promised Mom I would be home early so I can't afford to wait another twenty minutes for a bus."

"Okay, call me later." She kissed him. "I love you, Baby."

"Love you, too."

D-Money bounced down the steps and headed for Foothill Boulevard to catch the bus home. It was now dark and getting a little chilly so he zipped up the sweat jacket he was wearing. Pulling the hoodie over his head, he inserted plugs into his ears and listened to music while walking at a brisk pace so he would not miss the bus. Once he got close to the corner of Foothill, D-Money nearly collided with a dude running around the corner onto 26th.

Avoiding the collision, D-Money looked up and saw his bus roll right past him to its next stop on the corner of 27th. Breaking into a sprint, he crossed the street so occupied on catching it that he failed to see the police car screech to a halt with one of the officers jumping out running across the street behind him with his weapon drawn.

Haskins spotted the suspect running across Foothill in the opposite direction from which he and

Falherty were riding and since there was too much traffic for a u-turn, he jumped out giving chase. D-Money matched the description given of Spunk, wearing white tennis shoes, blue jeans, and a dark colored hoodie.

"Police, stop!" shouted Haskins.

With music blasting in his ears, D-Money could not hear any noise from the streets around him, but saw everyone looking behind him and backing out of the way. Haskins thought he was ignoring the command to halt and when he noticed the shiny object in D-Money's hand, stopped to take dead aim and fired. D-Money turned his head looking back to see what had everyone else's attention when the bullet struck him in the back. Falling face forward to the concrete, he was dead instantly as his cell phone slid harmlessly out of his hand a few feet in front of his body. Octavia Wilson had just walked out of the store across the street with her sister, Tamora, when she heard the gunshot. Wandering over to be nosy, she joined the crowd which had gathered near the body and screamed upon recognizing Demonte.

Haskins was busy searching his pockets looking for a weapon as Flaherty, who had witnessed the entire sequence of events scoured the area around Demonte's body. Octavia called Levitra's phone but was so incoherent in her speech that Tamora grabbed the phone from her explaining to Levitra what had just happened to Demonte.

"Why you kill Demonte?" Octavia shouted at Haskins. "He didn't do nothing" she cried.

"He had a gun," Haskins said to Flaherty.
"Looks like he was holding his cell phone."
Flaherty showed him the phone. "Did you
find the weapon?"
"I can't find it" shouted Haskins.

Out of nowhere, the crowd swelled to
hundreds of people and became unruly as several
patrol cars converged on the scene. Officer
Coleman and his partner, Joey Payton arrived and
moved slowly through the crowd to reach Haskins
and Flaherty. Looking Haskins directly in the eye,
Coleman spoke.

"We need to get you out of here. Come with
me," Coleman told Haskins.

Coleman led Haskins to his patrol car while
Flaherty and Payton stood guard over Demonte's
body. By now the street had turned to a mob scene
with instigators urging the crowd on, getting them
good and riled up.

"Them damn pigs keep killing all of our kids
for no god damn reason," one of them
shouted.

"Then lie and cover it up," hollered another.

"Maybe we need to start killing them for a
change," screamed a woman to the cheering
crowd.

One of the instigators spotted Haskins being led by
Coleman to a patrol car and promptly alerted the
crowd.

"There the bastard go," he pointed *at
Haskins, "*trying to sneak off."

"Let's go get that mother….." screamed
another.

The crowd converged on Coleman and Haskins who were now joined by other officers, and tried to prevent them from getting inside the patrol car. Officer Coleman was slowly forcing his way through the crowd to the squad car with people doing all they could to prevent it. By the time he and Haskins were safely inside, the mob began rocking the car from side to side in an attempt to turn it over.

Coleman eased on the gas inching through the crowd to safety as the residents of that community let loose a fury Haskins had never seen before. He had been a part of many protests against law enforcement, but never in the center with the object of their anger squarely on his shoulders. At that exact moment in his life, wondering whether or not he would make it out alive, Coleman no longer looked like a baboon to Haskins. He now saw the black man trying to protect him from an angry mob of blacks and Hispanics as a man, colored be blind.

Everyone knew Demonte "D-Money" Edwards was on his way to college with a full ride athletic scholarship so there was no way he would do anything criminal to jeopardize it. Whatever reason the police had killed him for, the troublemakers said, just had to be racism at work and the cop who pulled the trigger must be held accountable.

Once Demonte's mother, Karla, and his sister Kiana arrived on the scene with Levitra, the crowd's anger was fueled to an even higher level. They were led through the crowd to Demonte's now covered up body but the cops were preventing her from identifying her son until homicide detectives showed up.

Kiana Edwards was a carbon copy of her mother Karla, standing five-seven with the same milk chocolate complexion accented by high cheekbones as her brother. Blessed with soft brown eyes, pearl white teeth, and a medium-sized round nose on a lean angular face, she had nice sized breasts with shapely hips and a round behind.

When Levitra called them, they were just returning home from a church business meeting and still dressed in the clothes they had worn to work. With the streets full of angry residents, they opted to park at Levitra's house and walk/run around the corner shocked and surprised that police would not let them near the body.

Finally, they were allowed to get up close to Demonte's covered up corpse. Karla lifted up the tarp and wailed loudly in a scream only a mother could have for a slain child. It sent chills through the crowd as Octavia and Levitra tried unsuccessfully to console her. Kiana kneeled over her dead brother, crying just as loudly as her mother.

> "Demonte, get up!" Kiana screamed. "Why did they shoot him. He was just going home."
> "Why they kill my Baby?" Karla asked no one in particular. "He didn't do nothing wrong." She turned to the crowd of onlookers. "Which one did it?"
> "He had just left my house. He didn't try to rob no store" shouted Levitra for all to hear

Van loads of police arrived on the scene with the intent on restoring order to the streets. The crowd was in near riot mood and did as they always do with officer involved shootings, which was to organize, then head downtown to city hall. Marching down Foothill, oblivious to traffic and followed closely by cops, it would be a long night for all. Demonte's covered-up body remained on the street, waiting for homicide detectives to arrive and begin their investigation while Karla, Kiana, Octavia, Tamora, and Levitra, huddled nearby praying.

12

THE ASSIGNMENT

Darnell Oliver lay under the covers of his bed, getting the last bit of rest in before he would dress for his graveyard shift. His spot was a small nine hundred and eighty square foot, two-bedroom apartment located in the hills off Mountain Boulevard situated between Edwards and 98th Avenues above the 580 Freeway. Fully furnished, he rented the place on a monthly basis and paid the bill using overtime money.

Living in the San Joaquin County city of Manteca, Darnell refused to commute the two-hour journey to work each day. The side apartment allowed him to get the proper rest in between shifts and, being single, he felt there was no need to drive that far to go to an empty house. It also served as a sex pad where he would host wild parties with his cop buddies who wanted privacy when cheating on their wives.

With midweek off days of Wednesday and Thursday nights, he would often rent the spot to fellow cops who did not want to drive home to far away locales. Darnell was an only child and contrary to his outward, happy-go-lucky façade, was a loner by nature so living alone was not an issue. He had enjoyed the company of many beautiful women and felt life was good.

After graduating from college with a degree in Sociology, he found the pickings slim for well-paying jobs and decided to become a cop. It was a move he considered rewarding because it allowed him to collect all the toys which accompanied having a nice salary. He owned a boat, a car, a truck, a motorcycle, jet skis, and assorted electronic gadgets.

Still upset about the new overtime reduction mandate, he worried about keeping his bachelor pad, knowing full well the loss of income would strap him financially. Barry White's slow love song, "Turn out the Lights", played softly on his sound system as he stared at the dark ceiling. In two hours he would get up. Suddenly, his cell phone rang so he answered it without checking to see who was calling.

"Hello," he spoke into the phone.

"Good evening, Detective," the dispatch operator greeted. "You have been assigned to an officer involved shooting which just occurred on the corner of 27th Avenue & Foothill Boulevard. They request your immediate presence on the scene."

"Okay," he responded.

"Can you inform your partner, or should I?" she asked.

"I'll inform my partner," he answered.

"Okay, thank you."

"Bye." He ended the call.

Pulling the covers over his head, he cuddled up to the warm body next to him, gently massaging her luscious breasts.

"A case?" asked his partner, Coco Gutierrez.

"Yes," he answered. "Officer involved shooting on Foothill."

"Maybe we should get up, Honey?" She was concerned.

"Since they won't pay until we get there, we'll go at our normal time. You heard what the union rep told us today," he said.

"What are we going to do until then?" She sat up. "I can't go back to sleep now."

"You don't have to." He smiled.

Darnell began kissing Coco softly as the music played, slowly easing her back down onto the sheets. She hugged him tightly as he straddled her legs and plunged deep inside her body. Now she no longer cared about the phone call, or her husband for that matter. She only cared about pleasing her new man who could satisfy her like no one else.

13

INTERROGATED

The homicide office in police headquarters was small with sixteen detectives cramped inside one room. There was a tiny office for the Lieutenant and three interrogation rooms. Two of them had peepholes outside the door where detectives could look inside to check on suspects. The third room, which sat directly across from the Lieutenants office, had a large window covered by old worn out venetian blinds and a smaller window built into the door, also covered by blinds. That room was generally used for witnesses giving statements or to house suspects.

All three rooms had one table bolted to the floor. A set of handcuffs were welded on the side of the table, which was surround by three chairs. Suspects were routinely handcuffed to the table during their entire time in custody and had to eat bag lunches using only their free hand. When the need arose to use the restroom, they would have to bang on the table, shout at the top of their lungs, or for those with long legs—kick the door to get the attention of detectives.

Johnson and Wratney had spent all of Sunday night and long into the wee hours Monday morning questioning Scooty without success. No matter what tactic they used, be it good cop/bad cop, lying about evidence, or flat out intimidation, nothing worked and Scooty did not crack under pressure.

Once daylight hit and they had completed the equivalent of a double shift, they went home to get some much needed sleep and would return later to resume their interrogation of Scooty. Besides, they reasoned, he wasn't going anywhere.

Arriving back at the homicide office at a mutually agreed upon six in the evening, instead of their normal three o'clock reporting time, they reviewed notes and discussed strategies to be used on Scooty. Johnson checked with Sam Wang in the evidence unit to see if he had anything new to report while Wratney contacted the coroner's office for the same reason.

The next two hours were spent writing reports from the previous night's murders. Finally, after getting all of the preliminaries out of the way, they were ready to resume their questioning of Raphael "Scooty" Martin. Entering the interrogation room located at the back of the office, they found Scooty curled on top of the table in a fetal position sound asleep with his left wrist still handcuffed to the table. Johnson shoved him forcefully off the table and flung him back into the chair.

"You ready to tell us what you know?" barked Johnson.

"Man I told you I don't know nothing and you don't have to be pushing either."

"Okay, let's hear it from the top again. What happened at the shooting?"

"I told you I don't know about no shooting," answered Scooty. "Why you keep asking me the same thing? My story ain't gon' change."

"Oh, you'll tell me something." Johnson tried to rip the chair from beneath him.

"Like I said before, we was riding down Foothill, minding our own business when somebody started shooting. We was caught in the crossfire and I tried to speed away but Blue got hit, so I drove him to the hospital then called his Mother."

"Look, punk."

"I got yo punk all right, negro, you don't scare nobody." Scooty was defiant.

Wratney grab Johnson by the arm and pulled him from the room. He didn't like the direction this interrogation had taken because they had tried the intimidation route before. Closing the door behind them, he spoke to his partner.

"Calm down, Norman, don't let this jerk get under your skin," said Wratney.

"I know, Larry. It's just something about that guy that makes me want to knock him out."

The front door to the office opened with both detectives looking on as Sam Wang walked in with the trademark stoic expression on his face. They had no idea what Sam would say because his poker face gave no clues.

"Hey, guys," Sam greeted.

"Hope you got some good news," Wratney said.

"Better than that," Sam answered. "We searched the car your suspect was driving and found blood belonging to Eddie 'Day-Lo' Winston whose body was found under the bleachers at Mack High School this morning. We also lifted shell casings which match the ones taken out of both Banks and Roger's bodies. So whoever shot those two was definitely inside the car with Martin and had something to do with the murder of Winston."

"What about the gun?" inquired Wratney.

"No weapon was found but I was allowed to test the two shooting victim's hand's for gunpowder residue at the hospital."

"Find anything?" asked Johnson.

"Yes, the hands and clothes of Mario Barnes showed massive traces of residue. I also got his blood sample and am in the process of running a DNA test to see if it matches blood found in the car."

"Thanks, Sam," both men said in unison.

"No problem," Sam responded.

Sam walked out the door just as casually as he had entered with his blank facial expression. Johnson gave Wratney a high-five as both men now had a newfound attitude, which only moments earlier was not there. They now had solid evidence with facts to back it up and felt Scooty had no choice but to cooperate. Reentering the interrogation room, Wratney closed the door and spoke first.

"Okay, Martin. The game's over."

"What game?" Scooty asked with a frown on his face.

"We can prove whoever killed Hot Link and wounded Catfish, did the shooting from your car. We also found Day-Lo's blood in your vehicle, so either you're involved and did it, or you're covering for Blue. Now we don't care if you take the fall or not. You can carry the secret to your grave for all I care, but somebody's going to prison for this," Wratney promised.

"I want a lawyer. See what I'm saying?" Scooty growled.

"That's fine," said Wratney, "but you really need to take time and consider your options. You could be facing charges of first degree murder for the double homicides and attempted murder, or if you cooperate, you would be looking at less severe charges. So what's it going to be?"

"I ain't got nothing else to say, feel me?" Scooty said.

This time Johnson pulled Wratney from the room, watching angrily at Scooty, who smiled at them leaving. Before the door closed, Scooty once again curled up on the table in a fetal position to get some sleep, still handcuffed.

"Think he'll talk?" asked Wratney.

"He'd take the rap and get a life sentence before he talks, Larry. There is not much honor amongst thieves, but this dude is the poster child for no snitching. He'd die and go to hell before he told on Blue."

"Wow," said Wratney, "some kind of loyalty, huh?"

"He wears it like a badge of honor," stated Johnson.

"So since Blue definitely handled the gun--"

"Let's get a search warrant, then pay him a visit," Johnson said.

The detectives removed their jackets from the coat rack and were headed out the door when

Johnson's cell phone rang. The number displayed on his screen was from central dispatch.

"Johnson" he answered.

"Good evening, Detective," the dispatch operator greeted. "We need you and your partner to cover an officer involved shooting which just occurred on the corner of 27th Avenue & Foothill Boulevard."

"What about Oliver and Gutierrez?"

"They answered the call but have not arrived at the crime scene yet," she answered before continuing. "It has turned into a riot situation and the body still hasn't been moved."

"On our way," Johnson ended the call.

"What about Oliver and Gutierrez?" Wratney asked his partner.

"Well, they were assigned to an officer involved shooting but haven't arrived at the crime scene yet," answered Johnson.

"Wonder who shot somebody?" Wratney said out loud without an answer from Johnson.

The detectives now walked out the door with a different destination in mind. The assignment board, which was situated on the wall near the front entrance had Darnell and Coco in line for the next case. Both Johnson and Wratney wondered if the no show was due to their anger at the new overtime reduction rule. They hoped that was not the reason. Entering the hallway, they found the building nearly deserted which meant a riot was about to jump off. Now they really felt sorry for their fellow detectives.

"Hope they have a good reason," said Johnson.

"They'd better," answered Wratney.

14

OPPOSING SIDES

The crowd of protesters, who had marched down the middle of Foothill from 27th Avenue on the Eastside to the intersection of 14th & Broadway in the heart of downtown, had swelled from several hundred to several thousand. As people got word of the officer involved shooting by radio, television, or word of mouth, they hit the streets heading for protest spot ground central. That was the Civic Center Plaza which sat directly in front of City Hall.

Concerned residents of the city were joined by Black Lives Matter members, students from nearby Cal Berkeley, professional antagonists, and street thugs looking for an opportunity to steal. Police in response had deployed every available officer, setting up resistance lines to keep law and order yet allow a peaceful protest.

Included in the police group were the violence suppression unit, gang unit, vice squad, beat cops, and SWAT. It was the type of assignment desk sergeants hated because they had to change from suits into riot gear and man the streets right along with everyone else.

Like most protests, the event started out peacefully with law abiding citizens speaking their mind on a microphone, with their voices resonating through the crowd from privately owned sound systems. They were demanding justice and accountability from local officials to stop the unnecessary killing of unarmed black men.

Representatives from the news media were also out in full force, interviewing participants for newspaper stories and videotaping the activities for newscasts. Oaktown had gained a local and national reputation for protests beginning as far back as the sixties with the Black Panther Party.

More recently they had been known for the Occupy protests of two thousand eleven where during the middle of the night, cops unceremoniously raided the occupy camp discarding all personal possessions belonging to camp members. That show of force was replayed time and again on national newscasts around the country and gave the city a serious black eye in regards to sensitivity.

Amy Rouse was an onsite reporter for the local news and had covered the Occupy Movement protest for the entire year they camped out in Civic Center Plaza. For that in depth coverage which was fair and impartial, she was rewarded with a permanent assignment at City Hall. Although she preferred to be an anchor in the studio, Amy took the assignment with pride and was determined to be the best onsite reporter in the business.

Small in stature, Amy stood a mere five-two, yet possessed a very nice figure and appeared much taller on camera. She had a beautiful face with aqua blue eyes, a tiny nose, and small lips accented by candy apple red lipstick, which made them look fuller than they actually were.

Standing off to the side of City Hall away from the crowd, Amy rehearsed her lines repeatedly, determined to get it right. As she did so, people would walk behind her posing, throwing up gang signs, or basically acting like fools, thinking they would be seen on the news later that night or the next day. You could also hear the chants Black Lives Matter—Black Lives Matter, over and over again.

True to her profession, Amy was unfazed by the distractions and would continue practicing her report until she felt it was perfect. Once she was satisfied, she let her cameraman know that this take would probably be the one forwarded to the station. Straightening out her clothes and checking her makeup, she began.

> *"If you look behind me, you can see rioters trashing the city in protest of the latest officer involved shooting, which claimed the life of Demonte Edwards, a high school basketball star who had just received a full ride college scholarship. He was shot in the back while running for the bus after leaving his girlfriend's house. The community is in an uproar demanding answers from the police department, and city hall on what changes will be made to rid the department of its alleged rogue cops and shoot-first mentality."*

On cue, the camera showed people looting, destroying cars, smashing windows of businesses, and trying to get past police skirmish lines which resembled a tug of war match between protesters and cops.

> *"City officials have yet to respond to this latest incident and residents are demanding answers. We will keep you updated on any further*

developments as they occur. Reporting from City Hall, this is Amy Rouse"

On the third floor of City Hall, safe and secure inside his office, the Mayor, along with his Chief of Police, watched the shenanigans outside from an obscure location where they could see, but not be seen. Arthur Burkes was nearing the end of his first term as Mayor and desperately wanted to be re-elected for a second one.

He hated incidents such as this one because they tarnished his image which he had meticulously crafted as a man of the people. That image was only in his mind because residents in racially diverse neighborhoods such as Adams Point, Rockridge, Temescal, Trestle Glen, Montclair, and the hills considered him a complete failure who catered to the flatlands, which were dominated by people of color. Many of those upper income areas went as far as to hire private security firms to patrol their neighborhoods because they felt the police department ignored them.

Now the flatland residents were becoming frustrated and showed it by the numerous protests, which seemed to be occurring on a weekly basis. Mayor Burkes was a distinguished looking gentleman who stood six feet two on a lean and trim two-hundred-pound frame. He had a low cut salt and pepper afro with thick black eye lashes and a mustache. Soft brown eyes, a wide flared nose, and thick lips were set perfectly on his mocha-colored smooth face.

Having served on the City Council for over twenty years until term limits forced him out of office, he had been the lone spokesman for the black community. His unwavering representation was the sole reason he was highly respected by people of color. James Watson, on the other hand, was vilified in the flats as being a sellout.

Chief Watson had been on the force for nearly thirty years, slowly moving up the ranks to the role of Deputy Chief, which was second in command. Having been passed over numerous times for the top job, which was awarded at the sole discretion of the Mayor, he was more than elated when Burkes named him Chief.

Flatland residents considered it an insult and were extremely upset with the Mayor's selection because they felt Watson was one of the good old boys and did not have the guts to discipline rogue cops. Well-liked by the rank and file, fellow cops thought he was the perfect choice to lead them.

Watson also stood six feet two inches like the Mayor, on a solid two hundred and thirty-pound frame. With a clean shaven, cocoa brown skin complexion, he had a medium sized nose, and thin lips, which were uncommon for a black man. He also had jet black eyes which could drill a hole through you and was a no-nonsense type of guy.

The purpose of their meeting was for Chief Watson to divulge his strategy to Mayor Burkes so Burkes would not be left in the dark at the inevitable press conference. The last thing the Mayor needed was to be blindsided by questions he could not answer. Looking out the window at thousands of people saturating the plaza, Burkes spoke to Watson.

"What is your department doing about that?" Burkes demanded.

"We've set up a skirmish line on 13th to prevent them from marching to headquarters. For the college students lying down in the middle of 14th & Broadway in peaceful protest, we are diverting traffic to 12th, 15th, Webster, and MLK. The Black Lives Matter folks and anarchists trying to converge on the courthouse are being arrested on the spot, mostly for vandalism. It seems like they have stolen a page from the Occupy Movement," answered Chief Watson.

"Did you remind your people not to use excessive force? The city doesn't need any more lawsuits," said Mayor Burkes.

"We only use excessive force if nothing else works. Many of the protesters are not even city residents, just anarchists and troublemakers, looking to stir up the crowd."

"It seems like they're winning" said Burkes "and giving us a black eye in the process. You know I'm putting you front and center at the press conference so be ready. With the re-election coming up, this is the last thing I need. Why can't you control your officers, James? And give them some training?" Mayor Burkes yelled.

"Oh, hell, Arthur, you know my officers receive on-going training, in all aspects of police work and when incidents like this happen, before you jump on the public's bandwagon, at least let us complete our investigation," Chief Watson answered back just as loudly.

"You have until tomorrow morning," Burkes warned.

Mayor Burkes opened the door and stood by it, which Chief Watson knew meant the meeting was over. Watson walked out without even saying goodbye and did not flinch upon hearing the door slam behind him. Burkes picked up the phone and called his public information officer, instructing her to inform the media of a press conference at nine o'clock tomorrow morning.

Once again looking out of his office window, he saw the crowd of protesters trying to force their way past the police resistance line without success. Next, they turned around and began marching towards the Westside which meant one thing. They were headed for the 980 freeway located a mere three blocks away, and would take it over, disrupting innocent drivers from reaching their desired destinations.

The Mayor sat down with his elbows on the desk and hands covering his face. Suddenly he had a headache and felt this was definitely going to be a long night.

15

ISSUES

It was a somber mood engrossing the student body due to the death of Demonte Edwards. Grief counselors were onsite and available for students wishing to talk about how they felt or to release pent up anger, frustrations, and anxiety. The majority had witnessed death within their family or people they knew, but never up close and personal like now. D-Money was like family, someone who they saw and interacted with on a daily basis.

That made it much harder to take because he was one of them. Levitra and Octavia both had puffy eyes from crying all night, but decided on coming to school anyway to show support for Demonte. Basketball team members openly cried for their fallen teammate and now realized how fleeting life could be when compared to a game.

Demonte's death served as a wakeup call to every student on campus that your life, dreams, and plans could be over in an instant. As they drifted into their first period class, Mister Tucker sat at his desk eyeing each student closely to try and get a read on their mental state. He knew this would be a difficult day for all of them and planned to tread lightly. Before he could say a word, they brought the conversations from outside into the room.

"Man, he was going to college," said Bobby. "We were just talking about it the other day when D-Money said he was going far away to get away from this nonsense." He shook his head.

"Yes, he did," stated Lavelle. "At the time, we had no way of knowing that my boy was going to get shot by five-o. That's crazy, man, because D-Money was just here in class talking about most black dudes shot by the police usually were breaking the law. It's bad enough that every day we see people our age and younger around here killing each other for no reason. Then when the police start wrongly killing innocent people like they did Demonte." He paused for effect. "It all goes to a whole new level."

"That cop should be fired immediately," said JP. "He was the same creep who pulled us over for no reason."

"And kept staring at me and D-Money like we were common criminals," added Bobby.

The class grew silent so Mister Tucker remained quiet, too. After a couple of minutes, he finally addressed them.

"I think we can all agree that Demonte's passing is a terrible tragedy, which leaves us all at a loss for words. I do applaud you guys for showing up at school today and encourage you to keep your heads held high in support of his memory." He rose from his desk and continued. "I personally hurt not because he was one of my ballplayers, more to the point that he had his whole life ahead of him. Now, the lesson plan I had for today." He paused. "I tossed it in the trash. What I would like to do, if it's all right with you all, is to discuss some of the reactions to this tragedy."

The class remained silent as Tucker began pacing back and forth across the floor.

"Can someone tell me why the community reacts to officer involved shootings in the manner that they do?" he asked.

"What manner?" Bobby asked him.

"By rioting, looting, engaging in physical altercations with the police, destruction of property, marching onto the freeway."

"The community has to do something," Levitra said softly. "That stuff is bottled up inside and if we don't let it out, we'll go crazy. The police are always doing wrong by men of color. They see them from a stereotypical perspective as being menacing, illiterate, and violent. They'll stop you just for looking black," all of her classmates nodded in agreement.

"Maybe they do, Miss Gant, but my question is about how we act as a community after an officer involved shooting. And to stand on the other side of the fence for a minute—why don't we act that way when our neighbor gets shot by the thug down the street. In that scenario, everybody knows who did it, but nobody tells. There are no protests, no looting, just business as usual. Does anybody wish to respond?" he asked.

"The reason no one tells is because they still have to live here," spoke up JP. "See, once you tell, then the district attorney wants you to testify. Now that right there will get you killed."

"Even if you don't testify, their lawyer's tell them everything you said," chipped in Lavelle. "So they know. Then word hits the street that you're a snitch and that gets you killed."

"What can be done to change the culture?" Tucker asked. "What can be done to eliminate fear of the no snitching mentality?" Total silence, so Tucker continued. "How can the law-abiding citizens reclaim their neighborhoods?"

"Well, it's kind of happening right now on its own, but when it goes full circle, I know the politicians and police will be taking the credit for it" said Octavia.

"What is it that's happening right now, Miss Wilson?"

"Let me see if I can break it down so you can see where I'm coming from." Octavia paused to collect her thoughts. "You got Blacks and Mexicans moving out in droves to the suburbs like Antioch, Tracy, and Fairfield. What happens is they have a relative get a spot out there on Section 8 for the cheap. Then when they go visit to see it, they fall in love with the fact that they can rent a big giant house for twenty percent on the dollar. So what you have is a welfare recipient sitting in what is to them, a four or five-bedroom mansion, paying three-hundred-and-fifty dollars a month for rent instead of seventeen-fifty. Now if I can be real for minute, you got everybody and their Momma moving out to the suburbs. Shoot, all my cousins stay in Antioch. So what has happened is the whites and Chinese are slowly moving back here, and the city is fixing things up. The cost to rent a place to live has gone way up, they're hiring more police, and opening up a ton of charter schools. It's all going on, but most people don't see it happening. I bet those Yayhoos' in Antioch know crime done went up though" her classmates nodded agreement kill to Octavia's synopsis.

"So you believe the problem is fixing itself?"

"That's not exactly what I said" Octavia responded "the problem isn't being solved or addressed, it's just relocating to the suburbs but the politicians and police here will take credit for reducing crime. And for all the suburban homeowners who are stuck because they can't sell and move out, I feel sorry for them."

"Anybody else?" asked Tucker.

"I can say for a fact that some of those people don't care what the reason is," said Bobby. "If you give them any excuse, they're going to loot. It could be the Raiders making the super bowl...."

"WHEN?" shouted Lavelle, followed by roaring laughter from his classmates.

"Y'all know what I'm saying," Bobby said sheepishly. "They're going to loot and tear up stuff just because you made the super bowl. Then, win or lose, they'll do it again, and that goes double for police shootings."

"But why not for brown on brown killings Bobby?" Tucker asked.

"For the same reasons I said the other day," answered Bobby. "The police don't really care about our lives because they view us as being out here illegally anyway. What they need to do is change the way they operate and start firing some of the crooked cops. Everybody knows that police break all kind of rules but never get fired. That's why when they outright kill somebody in cold blood, all hell breaks loose. If they won't police themselves, we'll do it for them."

"Jeffrey, you've been quiet," Tucker looked at JP.

"My take focuses on police accountability," JP said. "They try to sweep everything under the rug, and it needs to stop. For example, this guy who killed D-Money, if he's a problem, you can bet your bottom dollar that boatloads of cops know that already. But now even though he should be facing severe disciplinary action, they'll let him off the hook and he'll run right back out there and do the same thing."

"You have any evidence or past history to back up that statement?"

"We don't need past history when you can see them doing it right now. The police are already trying to attack his character by saying he got into trouble four years ago behind drugs. And the media is eating it up like the suckers they are" JP was irate

"Oh, really? What happened?" Tucker was unaware of this bit of information.

"We were in Junior High and a group of us got suspended because some of them were smoking weed at the school dance. Since they couldn't prove who it actually was, and nobody snitched, they suspended all of us. Now the police got wind of it and are trying to portray D-Money as a pot head. Sneakily insinuating that he was a lawbreaker."

"The good old no-snitch policy," said Tucker. "Alive and well even in Junior High."

"From my time knowing D-Money, he wouldn't touch the stuff with a ten-foot pole," said

JP. "But even if he did, that has nothing to do with his murder. The renegade cop who shot him has several 'excessive use of force' complaints lodged against him, and this is not the first time he shot someone. As a matter of fact, when he stopped us Friday night with a phony excuse that my tail light was malfunctioning, which was a flat out lie, I knew he was rotten then."

The bell rang ending the class and students quietly gathered their possessions walking out. Mister Tucker followed them out the room heading next door to Diana Meadows class. She was standing outside her door, waiting, and upon seeing him approach, smiled broadly. They greeted each other with a handshake, then went inside to "chat" before heading to the auditorium. The principal had hastily called a school assembly to address students concerns regarding Demonte's death, so there would not be any second period classes. No one seemed to notice when those two entered fifteen minutes late, through separate doors.

16

THUGS

On Tuesday morning, Highland Hospital gave Catfish his release papers allowing him to go home and recuperate from his wounds. Johnson and Wratney surely would not like this bit of information because they never got around to questioning him about the shooting. Catfish was happy knowing they had been looking to speak with him, but medical staff had unknowingly provided the perfect cover saying he was too weak to talk when they had attempted to ask him questions.

Still too weak to move around, he would require bed rest and medications for the next several weeks. This didn't sit too well with him because he wanted to exact revenge on the people who shot him and killed his boy, Hot Link. They would most definitely have to pay.

The apartment he lived in was located on 35th Avenue, a very busy thoroughfare situated between Penniman and Fleming on the eastside. Built in a u-shape with the parking lot in front, the complex was a Section 8 facility painted off-yellow with brown trim. A magnet for crime, drug dealing, and usage due to the high unemployment rate of its tenants, the place was cool with Catfish.

His girlfriend, Marvette, had picked him up from the hospital and would have the job of nursing him back to health. She had been his steady woman for three years and was already the mother of two when they became a couple. Add in two more crumb snatchers fathered by him and the end result was six people piled into a three-bedroom apartment.

Marvette Collins had a nicely-shaped body and loved putting it on display by wearing hip-hugging stretch pants or painted on jeans with snug halter tops. With hips, butt, and large breasts, she would turn many heads when walking down the street until you saw her mug. Everything above the neck was ugly, starting with rotten and chipped teeth greeting you whenever she opened her mouth.

Her hair was nonexistent due to putting too many hot combs on it as a youngster and burning it up. She wore wigs of the cheap variety, which always seemed to be on crooked. Her lips were larger than those on a horse and more red than brown, due to heavy alcohol consumption on a daily basis by her and Catfish. Marvette's face had many scars and scratches from the fights she had with other women and Catfish.

Theirs was a love/hate relationship, generally based on how much money was in their pockets. When the money was flowing, they loved each other, but when their funds were low, all hell broke loose. Ten years her junior, Catfish took the good with the bad because one thing was certain. He loved him some Marvette.

Taco and T-Bone were waiting in the parking lot when Catfish and Marvette drove up. They helped him up the stairs into the apartment and into his room as Marvette brought them chairs from the dining room table to sit on. Leaving the men alone, she went next door to get their two children who were not in school from a neighbor.

"What's up, boy?" asked Taco. "How you feeling?"

"I'm good, man. Glad to be outta dare," answered Catfish.

"You know why we couldn't visit, don't you?"

"Yeah, I know," he responded. "Five-o was all around, man. Ya boy Johnson and Wratney tried to come in dare but the nurses wouldn't let 'em." Catfish laughed. "Told those two fools I was too weak to talk. Shoot, I wasn't gone tell them nothing anyway."

"Man, did you see those fools roll up on you?" asked Taco.

"Man, they just rolled up on me and Link popping caps before we had a chance to move, dude."

"Yeah, Bro, we gone get them fools though," Taco promised.

"I just hate I didn't kill Blue that night, dog, but I am gonna finish the job next time."

"Blue?" Catfish asked. "Who is Blue?"

"Man, dass a fool I was in jail wit'," answered T-Bone. "Yaw bumped off his brother, Red, the other night. Negro used to walk around in da pen like he Mike Tyson or somebody; never came at me dough cause he know what time it is."

"Oh, Okay," Catfish said, "that explains it den." He stroked his chin.

Normally most guys boasting like T-Bone had just done would not be taken serious, but his partners knew he meant every word. Terence "T-Bone" Mayfield was built just as solid and muscular as Blue, with just as large a reputation. Coming from opposite sides of town, the rivalry developed naturally during their time spent in San Quentin Prison.

T-Bone was tall at six-three and weighed roughly two-forty. He was handsome with hazel eyes and a peanut butter skin complexion complimented by a body builder's physique. Well educated, he spoke Ebonics with his road dogs who considered the use of proper English talking like a white boy.

"Heard that yo Momma gave his Momma a beat down at the hospital." T-Bone smiled.

"Yeah, they say she pulled all that broad's weave off her head while upper cuttin' her like she was Tyson or somebody," Taco chipped in.

"Man, y'all know Momma always be tryin to be gangsta anyway. I'm in there dying and she out in the lobby acting a damn fool. Surprised old Johnson and Wratney didn't arrest her behind. You know those two fools be taking that five-o stuff way too serious." He got serious. "So I won't y'all to wait before you cap those fools."

"Wait for what?" Taco asked loudly.

"Cause I wanna be dare, Dawg," Catfish answered.

"Man, you know we can't wait til you heal up, man," said T-Bone. "Everybody'll thank we soft by den,"

"We gotta strike those fools right now, dude, and you know it," commented Taco.

"I know, man," Catfish said. "I just wanted to surprise them like they did me and Link."

"We got that covered, Boy," Taco promised.

"Word in da hospital was dat fool can't even walk," said Catfish.

"Yeah, I heard that, too," stated T-Bone. "Say dat fool gone need hella surgeries, see what I'm sayin?"

"You got that negro good, dawg," Taco gloated.

"But I only get a B-plus cause the job didn't get finished."

"Well, y'all ain't got to look too far cause his behind laid up just like me," grinned Catfish.

"We gone finish it today. Come on Bone," Taco ordered.

Taco and T-Bone rose to leave giving Catfish the pound fist over fist bump then headed out the room with the chairs they had been sitting on. Marvette entered as they were leaving giving each man a brief hug on the way out. Pulling out his pain pills from the bag supplied by the hospital, she grabbed two cold beers from the refrigerator and headed for the room. Her children were still at the neighbor's crib so she and her man would get their groove on, not caring that medicine and liquor don't mix.

17

TOWN HALL

In response to the officer involved shooting, which claimed the life of Demonte Edwards, a town hall meeting was called by the Mayor's office. Faced with enormous pressure from his constituents for the actions of police, Mayor Burkes had to show them that he was taking the matter seriously. He could not afford to let the chief of police be the face people saw leading the charge for reform.

Assuming correctly that hundreds, if not thousands, of people would attend, Mayor Burkes chose to have the meeting at a large venue which could house the masses. Normally town hall meetings were held at recreation or community centers, but tonight the event would take place at the Scottish Rite Center.

The Scottish Rite Center sat on the shores of Lake Merritt in the heart of the city, just a few blocks away from downtown. Various events were held there such as weddings, ballroom dancing, receptions, concerts, and high school graduations. The auditorium could hold up to fifteen hundred people, which the Mayor felt would be sufficient.

Uniformed police officer's lined the walls, lobby, and stage area inside the auditorium. Outside, they directed traffic and displayed a heavy law enforcement presence in order to dissuade troublemakers from creating havoc. None of them wore riot gear, by order of the Chief, as to not look intimidating or ready for a confrontation.

Representatives of the media were out in full force, both inside and outside, seeking stories from anyone of whom they deemed important. Several of the city's most prominent preacher's had been invited by the Mayor to join him on stage in a show of solidarity. Most arrived with large numbers of parishioners from their churches.

Once the doors opened, the center filled rapidly to capacity, resulting in the fire chief announcing to the hundreds still outside that no one else would be allowed entrance. In a brilliant stroke of pre-planning by the Mayor's staff, giant big screen television monitors with concert sized speakers were placed on both ends of the outer steps where everyone could view the meeting going on inside.

It was a concert like atmosphere around the perimeter with people selling 'Justice for Demonte' and 'Black Lives Matter' t-shirts, along with incense, perfumes, gift baskets, and snacks. Joining the Mayor and handpicked members of the Clergy onstage were top police officials and city council members representing each district. Amy Rouse had been selected by the Mayor to moderate the event and stood at a podium off to the side of the stage. On cue from Mayor Burkes, she called the meeting to order.

"Good evening, everyone," Amy greeted. "we have been invited to this town hall meeting courtesy of Mayor Burkes to discuss the mounting issues within our community. We ask that you should show respect to the speakers and refrain from using vulgar language. My name is Amy Rouse and I will serve as moderator. Without further adieu, I present to you Mayor Burkes."

Amy remained standing at her smaller podium as the Mayor slowly rose from his seat shaking hands with a few of the dignitaries on stage. Scattered boos from disgruntled protesters were drowned out by loud cheers from his supporters as Burkes walked up to the larger podium center stage.

"Thank you, Amy," he began, "we are here tonight for the purpose of bringing clarity to you, the community, regarding issues in our city which affect us all. I will start by saying we are conducting a comprehensive investigation into the shooting of Mister Demonte Edwards…"

"Comprehensive investigation?" shouted a heckler in the crowd "Comprehensive by who? Those crooked ass cops on your corrupt police force? We want an independent investigation by somebody who's not on your got-damn payroll." Elijah Collar, who was pastor of the largest black church in the city, tapped the Mayor on the shoulder then stepped to the microphone.

"Mister Mayor, if I may address the crowd?" he asked.

Mayor Burkes nodded, "yes,' and returned to his seat as Reverend Collar took his place. The crowd became silent and the heckler sat down, knowing better than to disrespect a person with the stature of Reverend Collar. He was the elder statesman amongst Baptist ministers and treated like a rock star.

Approaching sixty years of age, Reverend Collar looked ten years younger and was in good physical condition. He had a clean shaven face with a smooth caramel complexion and was dressed to a tee, sporting an expensive blue designer suit with matching Steve Harvey shoes. Speaking in what sounded more like a Sunday morning sermon than a town hall meeting, he began.

"Now what we would like is justice for *De-mon-te*... but we also have to play by the rules my people .... First, I would ask that we refrain from using foul language .... You can be upset ... *and verbalize it* ... without cursing somebody out ..... We're all upset about our kids being repeatedly shot down in cold blood .... Shot down by the very people paid to protect us .... But burning down businesses... looting ... beating up innocent citizens in the name of *De-mon-te* ... that ain't the way to go about it ...... The world is watching us act a fool ... like we have no home training ... animals, they call us ....Then they get to wondering... just like I do ...why come we don't have this much passion..."

Members of his congregation were shouting 'Amen' throughout his sermon.

".... And I say "why come" we don't have this much passion ..... When our children kill each other on a daily basis, like it's the thing to do .... Where is the protesting to that? .... Now I didn't come here to preach .... *but I will if I have to* .... Since my time is up, I'm going to turn the mike over to the Chief of Police and request that you give him the same respect you just gave me.... Amen."

The crowd responded with a loud "Amen" and a partial standing ovation as Reverend Collar returned to his seat, wiping off sweat with a silk handkerchief. Chief Watson stepped up to the podium for his turn.

"Thank you, Reverend Collar, for those eloquently spoken words….."

"Excuse me, Chief Watson," Amy interrupted.

"Yes, Amy?" he responded.

"I am not certain if anyone told you, but there has been a change to the format we are going to use for this meeting."

"A change?" Watson inquired.

"Yes, Sir. Instead of the normal report by you, then fielding of a few questions from us media people followed by comments from the public. I have been appointed by the Mayor and City Council as moderator and will ask you questions received from the audience on their way in. This way we feel everyone will get to have their say and we can avoid a chaotic scene which would accomplish nothing. Do you have any problems with this format, Sir?"

"None at all," Watson said.

If looks could kill, Mayor Burkes would have been dead on the spot because Chief Watson's eyes shot daggers straight through him. The Mayor appeared oblivious to him, looking in the opposite direction to avoid his mean mugging.

"First question, what is being done to address the 'use of excessive force' complaints against your rank and file?" she asked. "A number which is amongst the highest in the country."

"Our officers receive continuous training in all aspects of police work. In regards to excessive force, we conduct civil disobedience tactical training ..."

Amy interrupted him.... "Does this disobedience training include the use of tear gas, rubber bullets, flash bang grenades, and other non-lethal weapons?"

"I cannot answer your questions if you interrupt before I'm done responding Amy. Like I said, our officers are trained continuously in all aspects of police work which include the use of non-lethal crowd control weapons."

"Okay, how will your office investigate the latest officer involved shooting which took the life of Demonte?" she asked.

"I have been informed that the FBI will be conducting an investigation independent of our own internal investigation. After that, the grand jury will review the findings and decide whether or not to indict the officer involved."

"So your department will do an investigation anyway?" she made his statement sound ridiculous.

"Yes," he answered.

"Don't you think by doing an internal investigation, you'll get in the way of the FBI?"

"Not at all," he said.

"You state that your officers are trained in all aspects of police work, yet your department remains among the highest in the nation for officer involved shootings, which almost always end in death. Many times, like in the case of Demonte Edwards, the victim is an innocent person killed by a trigger happy cop. What kind of training are you giving these people? Please be specific," she said.

"Every three days there is a murder in our city. Nearly eighty percent of the time it's black on black, yet blacks make up only forty-six percent of the city's population. In many areas it's a war zone, and as police officers, we are on the losing end of that battle due to citizen's being uncooperative. By that I mean refusing to testify when they know who, what, when, where, why, and how it occurred. Occasionally, an officer is involved in a shooting, but, for the most part, the person shot was engaging in some sort of illegal activity."

Once again the instigator jumped to his feet shouting.

"You moron, Demonte wasn't engaged in nothing but going to college. Just like I always say, they always prop up an Uncle Tom negro like you to do their dirty work"

"Sir if you would please take your seat?" the Chief demanded

"Screw you" the heckler responded then sat down

"Like Reverend Collar was saying" Watson continued "where is the passion when blacks are killing blacks every day and nobody sees nothing, even though fifty people are standing right there when it happens?" he asked.

"Next question," Amy said. "What are you doing to rid your department of rogue cops?"

"Any officer on my staff that engages in illegal or criminal behavior is prosecuted to fullest extent of the law. We have zero tolerance for it."

Once again the instigator jumped to his feet.

"You a damned lie," he screamed. "Hell, Internal Affairs be protecting those sorry fools and you know it."

"Sir, could you please return to your seat?" Watson was angry.

"I ain't returning to nothing," he shouted. "Come make me," he challenged.

Two uniformed officers began to physically remove the heckler when suddenly and without warning, the woman sitting next to him slugged one of the cops.

"Let my damned Brother go," she hollered.

Instantly, chaos erupted as the two cops became engaged in violent wrestling matches with the siblings as other cops rushed to their aid. Many protesters who came with the sole intent of causing trouble joined in the melee as law abiding citizens ran for the exits. The Mayor, Council Members, and Clergy quietly exited through a side door while Amy Rouse's cameraman caught the entire episode on tape.

She would immediately record her narrative and have it spliced into the fracas, where it would be shown to the world within minutes. Yet again,

Oaktown would receive a black eye in the court of public opinion.

18

CONSEQUENCES

By the time Darnell Oliver and Socorro Gutierrez arrived on the scene where Demonte Edwards had been killed, Johnson and Wratney had already wrapped things up. When they returned to headquarters to find the precinct nearly deserted, they spent the remainder of the night following up leads on unsolved cases.

After leaving work, Coco spent another night with him making passionate love. Her excuse to her husband was built in because he had seen the news and knew the drill that all available staff was required to work the riot. Feeling refreshed after making love throughout the morning, they both were giddy and full of laughter.

Having spoken to their union rep and being assured that they had not broken any rules by showing up at their required reporting time, they felt there was nothing to worry about. Waiting for them upon their arrival was Captain Frazier, who was not smiling.

"You two in my office," Frazier ordered, "in ten minutes."

Frazier marched out the room leaving those two looking miffed. They knew he could not discipline them and wondered why he would want to rake them over the coals. Ten minutes later, they waltzed into the Captain's basement office. Closing the door behind them after entering, Oliver spoke first.

"What's up, Captain?" he asked.

"You two have been transferred effective immediately. Here is your written notice." He handed each one their transfer papers.

"Transferred?" asked Oliver.

"To where?" questioned Coco.

"Internal Affairs," answered Frazier.

"INTERNAL AFFAIRS," they said in unison.

"You know we are supposed to receive a ten-day written notice Captain before any transfer can take place, per the MOU," stated Oliver.

The MOU, short for Memorandum of Understanding, was a written agreement between the city and union negotiated upon during contract renewal. It contained every issue that could possibly occur on the job including attendance, vacation usage and accrual, medical leave, on the job injury, sick leave usage and accruals, disciplinary actions, so on and so forth. Employees considered it their Bible, and would pull out or cite the MOU for any and all disagreements with management.

"Can I ask why?" Oliver questioned.

"I'm not really sure, Darnell," Frazier lied.

"You know something, Captain," growled Coco.

"Look, when you guys chose not to respond in a timely manner to an officer involved shooting, a lot of folks wanted to know why detectives assigned to a case, which is very high profile, didn't show up, causing the case to be assigned to another team"

"Sounds like retaliation if you ask me," said Coco.

"Let's be real, Captain," said Oliver, "you know why we didn't come right away."

"I have an idea, but only you two really know why," Frazier lied again. "If it's behind the overtime reduction rule, you and Gutierrez screwed yourselves. That case needed to be investigated right away and you two were nowhere to be found. All eyes were on the department."

"Just so you know, we're taking it to the union," promised Coco.

"You can't file a grievance over a change in work assignments."

"We can when we haven't received due process by giving us a ten-day transfer notice," said Coco.

"And when the reason for the change is retaliation" added Oliver "we broke no departmental policies yet are being punished."

"You may have a point there, but until you file that grievance, they will expect you to report to IA tomorrow morning."

Oliver and Gutierrez looked at each other shaking their heads in disgust. Frazier thumbed through a stack of papers on his desk. After the moment of silence, the conversation continued.

"Can I ask you a question," Oliver spoke.

"By all means," answered Frazier.

"Did you request this transfer?"

"It came from higher up," Frazier said.

"Good, I'm glad you're just the messenger."

"Why is that?" Frazier asked.

"Because this will probably get ugly, and we've always thought of you as a stand-up guy."

"Thank you," said Frazier.

Oliver and Gutierrez shook the Captain's hand then walked out. They were headed back to the union office to file a grievance then to the spot for sex before Coco went home. Frazier picked up the phone and called his Human Resource partners to alert them of a soon-to-be filed grievance.

19

RETRIBUTION

It was a festive morning at the drug spot on Myrtle Street due to the fact Blue was home from the hospital. The street was highly populated with people engaged in various illegal activities, which was not unusual for this neighborhood on a weekday. Adults were drinking, smoking blunts, gambling, and selling dope to fiends seeking a fix.

Tasha sat on the front porch with her girls, Domonique and Symone, sharing a joint of weed and drinking forties of Old English straight from the bottle. Inside the crib, Scooty lounged on the loveseat while Blue stretched on the sofa. They too were smoking weed watching the Maury Povich Show, laughing loudly at the antics of his guests.

Blue had no idea that only five minutes after he had been released, Johnson and Wratney were at the hospital to arrest him. Their call out by central dispatch to fill in for Oliver and Gutierrez on the Barnes case prolonged their arrival at Highland. Once they got there and found he had been released, they knew they had screwed up big time.

Protocol would normally have them alert the officers on duty to arrest and handcuff him to the hospital bed but their egos got in the way. They wanted to be the arresting officers because that always looked good on your record, another notch in the belt so to speak.

Scooty had been just as lucky as his road dog because even though blood was found inside his vehicle, none of it was a match to him which meant they could not place him at the murder scene. Any lawyer worth his weight in gold would successfully argue that he could have loaned his car out to someone. Without a clear picture of his face in the Explorer when dropping Blue off at the hospital, they had to let him go.

"Word on the street is T-Bone shot me," Blue said, passing the weed. "That's just like that coward, never wanting to rumble when we was in the pen."

"Yeah, we got to kill da fool fa dat," Scooty said.

"No doubt," Blue agreed. "I'm still trippin off Momma fightin at the hospital though." They laughed.

"Man, you shoulda been dare, she whupped the dress off that broad." They both roared. "Ole girls bald headed butt was stannin dare in her stanky draws, talkin' crazy while Momma holding her dress and done scratched a tic-tac-toe board on her mug." They laughed again. "You know they say the apple don't fall too far from the tree." He cheesed choking on the weed before passing it back.

"What you trying to say, fool?" Blue was smiling.

"I see where you get yo crazy from now?" Scooty laughed heartily.

"Aw go ta hell, negro." Blue laughed louder than Scooty.

Outside, no one seemed to pay much attention to the slowly cruising black Charger rolling down the block. Probably some fool trying to spot their dealer amongst the crowd, most people thought. T-Bone scanned the crowd searching out Blue.

"That fool ain't out here," he said to Taco.

"That the house?" Taco asked.

"Yeah, das it," T-Bone answered.

Without warning, Taco lifted his AK-47 from the floor board and pulled the trigger, spraying bullets at anything moving. People dove and scattered in all directions to avoid being hit and for those aiming their own weapons, they were blown full of holes by Taco's rapid fire assault rifle. T-Bone had one hand on the steering wheel guiding the vehicle as his free hand fired off rounds from his own assault rifle into victims on his side of the street.

Satisfied with their work which took no more than a minute, yet left several people dead and many more wounded, T-Bone burned rubber getting out of there. Tasha, who had ducked for cover, crawled inside the house where she found both Scooty and Blue dead in the spots where they had been lounging.

Letting out a ground-shaking scream, she ran into the bedroom to retrieve a weapon then went back out on the porch. Police and ambulance sirens could now be heard in the distance rapidly approaching after the dispatch center received multiple calls for assistance. Symone rolled over on the porch shaking from the trauma of the incident, yet suffered only a superficial wound which had grazed her leg.

However, when Tasha called out for Domonique to get up, she did not move. She was killed instantly, having suffered several bullets to the head and face. The enormity of losing both of her brother's within a week, plus her lover left Tasha trembling to the core. The gun she was holding fell harmlessly on the porch as she cradled Domonique crying uncontrollably.

Symone managed to get up and take the gun back inside the house where she hid it under the sofa and Blue's dead body. Hobbling back out onto the porch, she waited for paramedics to give medical treatment to her wound and to comfort Tasha. All told, there were seven people killed and twelve injured. It was a very bloody morning.

When police questioned witnesses for their accounts of what had taken place, and who may have did it, they received the same answer from everyone involved. That was, "I don't know," which left cops speechless. Only this time, cops did not understand that the refusal to cooperate was not due to the no-snitching rule, more of the "we will handle it ourselves" creed of the streets.

20

Early Wednesday morning, Reggie McFadden stood on the front steps of City Hall, anxiously waiting for the media to set up their cameras. He had called a press conference to announce a wrongful death lawsuit filed against the city and its police department by the family of Demonte Edwards. Well known throughout the country as one of the finest civil rights attorneys in the state, if not the country, McFadden was in his environment.

He loved suing the city and serving as the unofficial watchdog over their police force. Most cops hated his guts and considered him nothing more than an ambulance chaser looking to make a quick buck. However, they did grudgingly respect him due to his outstanding win percentage in court. An excellent trial lawyer, McFadden viewed the courtroom as his theater and was highly animated when questioning witnesses on the stand.

Thirty-nine years old and the owner of a successful law firm, McFadden was a regular fixture on the local news, serving in the role of legal expert. With a flair for the dramatic, he enjoyed being in the limelight and got extreme satisfaction in making the police department look corrupt. Methodical in his approach, he routinely stretched the truth or exaggerated facts in order to win his cases.

Whenever citizens felt they had been mistreated, Reggie McFadden's office was generally the first place they called for advice. After having staff review the merits of their complaint, he happily accepted the job of representing them if he thought they had strong enough evidence to warrant a lawsuit.

McFadden was a short man, standing a mere five-eight on a slightly overweight two-hundred-pound body. His skin tone was in the shade of semi-sweet dark chocolate and his smile could light up a room. It was a broad grin stretching across his face which he displayed often. He had jet black eyes and a peanut shaped head with a low cut hairdo.

A very stylish dresser, he wore a grey pin striped double-breasted suit with matching shoes, powder blue button down shirt with cuff links at the wrists, and blue necktie complemented by a blue hanky poking out prominently from his upper coat pocket. He always wore hats to cover his long head and today was no different with him sporting a grey fedora with blue and white feather.

Flanking him on the right at the microphone was Karla Edwards, her husband George, and their daughter Kiana, all wearing dark sunglasses. George Edwards was dressed in a dark blue suit with matching shoes and pocket hanky. His white shirt was accented by a navy blue necktie. Judging from his appearance, one would never guess he worked as a school custodian because it did not fit the stereotypical which came with the profession.

To the right of McFadden stood Reverend Collar, there in support of the Edwards family, who were members of his church. As usual with anything relating to City Hall, Amy Rouse stood off to the side rehearsing her lines while her video crew recorded all activity going on around them.

A small group of people gathered in front of the steps, some who were in support of the family, and others simply passing by on the way to work. Noticeably absent was Black Lives Matter members whom McFadden failed to notify for fear of confrontation which would take away from the message. Also absent was the usual heavy police presence with only the two uniformed officers regularly assigned to City Hall posted inside the building, looking out the front entrance window.

Mayor Burkes and Chief Watson, along with members of the Mayor's staff were situated in his third floor office and would view the proceedings from his office window. The Mayor secretly would have loved to be out front and center because that would represent possible votes in the fall election. However, his position as Mayor meant he had to remain impartial.

Stepping up to the microphone, McFadden began the press conference.

"This morning a lawsuit was filed against the city and their police department on behalf of the family of Demonte Edwards. To lose your only son in the manner that the Edwards family lost Demonte is totally unacceptable, and even though no amount of money will be able to bring him back, we feel like the city and its police department must be held accountable. I warn you that we will be paying close attention to the Grand Jury, FBI, and OPD during their investigations to make sure they are conducted honestly and above board"

McFadden paused for a moment to let his words sink in and pose for photos from the many cameras taking pictures. He also glanced upwards to the Mayor's office window frowning as he returned his attention back to the crowd.

"The Edwards family has also hired an independent firm to conduct their own investigation into the senseless murder of Demonte and other young black and Latino men. They will review departmental patterns of racial discrimination and racial profiling, and the use of their stop and frisk policy. We feel the police department needs a major overhaul from the top down and this belief has given us a new mission and purpose. That is to make sure the necessary changes are made, hopefully without police running interference trying to stop everything we do."

"What sort of changes are you referring to Mister McFadden?" asked Amy.

"I'm referring to the elimination of police brutality, falsification of reports, outright lying on the witness stand, corruption – it's all about to come to a head," he stated.

Reporters began barking out questions, but McFadden ended the press conference. He had no interest in answering any of them because he knew any misstatement could come back to haunt him. As people walked away, Amy started recording her report in earnest. It would only receive a thirty second sound bite on the news due to the lack of drama, but she would file it anyway because that was her job.

21

THE CHASE

Johnson and Wratney arrived for duty early Wednesday morning with the sole purpose of tracking down Blue for the murder of Hot Link and Day-Lo. They were still upset that they had let him slip through the cracks, and knew they could only blame themselves for sloppy police work. With a crew of three patrol units joining them, they would raid his known address on Myrtle Street then his mother's house after that if necessary. For the manhunt, they were dressed in uniforms instead of suits and driving a patrol car.

As they rolled down West Grand crossing Market, they heard rapid fire gunshots which they knew were coming from an AK-47 assault rifle. Just as they hit Myrtle Street, a black Dodge Charger flew past them in the opposite direction at a very high rate of speed. Wratney maneuvered a u-turn and began a Code 2 pursuit, which in police lingo means lights flashing and sirens screaming. On cue, an operator from central dispatch came over the radio system.

"All units in the vicinity of Myrtle Street and West Grand, multiple reports of gunshots fired with many dead and wounded, suspect's vehicle described as late model black Dodge Charger, two or more suspects should be considered armed and dangerous.

"Unit 44 in pursuit," replied Johnson, "suspects are headed south on Market towards 14th Avenue."

T-Bone noticed the police car hit a u-turn and give chase so he hit the gas doing eighty miles an hour on city streets, running red lights and narrowly missing other cars. At 18th Avenue he hooked a left barreling down the street toward the 980 freeway.

"Suspects heading down 18th Avenue," shouted Johnson into the radio. "Cut him off at the Castro Street on-ramp."

As T-Bone approached the 18th & Castro intersection, he made a wide turn on Castro nearly losing control of the car. There was a large Chevron gas station on the corner which saved him because he ran over the curb onto the service station lot and continuing to drive like a maniac, sped onto the freeway.

"Suspects merging onto I-980," yelled Johnson into the radio " alert CHP"

Immediately after merging onto the 980, T-Bone had a choice, take the 580 to the deep eastern part of town, stay on 980 to Berkeley, or choose 580 West for Richmond / San Francisco. He chose the first option heading east to their neighborhood. Upon merging with eastbound traffic, T-Bone began to zigzag past slower drivers at speeds reaching one hundred miles an hour.

"Look up there, Man," hollered Taco.

What they noticed was the highway patrol had set up a road block. CHP Officers were positioned behind their cars with weapons drawn. With no other options available, T-Bone flew down the off ramp at Grand Avenue losing control crashing into several unsuspecting motorists as he attempted a right hand turn.

"Passenger's bailing," Wratney shouted to Johnson. "Driver, too."

"I got him, you get the driver," Johnson told his partner.

Taco jumped out running with Johnson on his heels.

"Stop, Police!" Johnson yelled at Taco.

Taco turned around firing a few rounds at Johnson who returned fire at him, with both men missing the mark. Realizing he was out of bullets, Taco tossed the gun into some bushes and jumped a fence running through the back of an apartment complex on Vernon Avenue. Johnson followed suit slowly gaining ground, as Taco hurdled several fences.

With Johnson now less than ten feet away, Taco ran around the corner of an apartment building and when Johnson followed suit, Taco stuck out a leg tripping the detective. Johnson fell to the ground looking on helpless as his gun slid in front of him. Taco seized the opportunity running to get the weapon but Johnson was up meeting him at the spot.

The two began furiously wrestling for control when suddenly the gun went off. Taco slumped over falling with a thud on the pavement, dead. Out of nowhere a crowd appeared with angry looks on their faces. There was a teenager coming from the store who had witnessed the chase and saw Taco toss the weapon. Walking over casually to the bushes, he shoved the weapon inside his pants and went home.

> "Dispatch, I'm going to need back up units along with the coroners van on Vernon Street right off Grand." Johnson spoke into the radio transmitter on his collar, "Tell them to make it quick."

> "Ten four, Sergeant," responded the

operator.

Within seconds, Officer Coleman and several other cops arrived and began to cordon off the area along with controlling the crowd. Back at the crash scene, T-Bone was dazed and struggling to get out of the car. Wratney reached inside grabbing T-Bones weapon with his own gun pointed directly at T-Bones head. Jerking him roughly from the car, Wratney flung him onto the hood of his police cruiser.

> "You're under arrest. You have the right to remain silent. Anything you say can and will be used against you in a court of law...."

Wratney continued reading T-Bone his Miranda Rights as he gently placed the still groggy suspect inside the back of his patrol unit. Over the radio he heard the dispatcher announce an officer involved shooting and knew instantly that Norman had bagged his man.

22

HOMEWORK

Students arrived for school still buzzing from the town hall meeting they had attended the night before. The majority had worn custom 'Justice for Demonte' black t-shirts or white tees with his photo and a familiar RIP, short for Rest in Peace, caption emblazoned on them. They came out in full force for their fallen classmate and were surprised by the conduct they had witnessed from adults.

The wild melee, which effectively ended the event shortly after it had begun, was the main topic of conversation described by students to those who were not there to witness it in person. The entire brawl was recorded by many on their phones and immediately posted on YouTube before they had even left the Scottish Rite Center.

Word spread around campus rapidly allowing the majority of administrators, faculty, and staff an opportunity to watch video upon arrival at the school. Most adults had saw brief footage on the morning news while getting ready at home, but did not get the full understanding of what truly took place until viewing it on YouTube.

As early arriving students drifted into the Current Events first period class, Thaddeus Tucker and Diana Meadows were viewing the tape on his computer. Tucker, who would use this for a future lesson plan, was writing down notes onto a sheet of paper. Meadows sat next to him with a look of shock on her face. In her world, you just didn't fight the police.

With more students wandering into the room, Tucker escorted Meadows to her own class where she could prepare to greet her students. Going to the main administration office to retrieve messages and mail, he stopped repeatedly to engage in small talk with fellow teachers and staff.

By the time he returned to his classroom, it was nearly full with the last stragglers easing in just as the tardy bell rang.

"Good morning, class," he greeted.

"Good morning, Mister Tucker," they greeted back.

"I had a chance to view the video from last night's town hall meeting and must say, it was truly an event to remember."

The class erupted with conversation as the ones who were there resumed giving the ones who were not their version of the melee.

"Okay, listen up everyone, let me have your attention" Tucker halted the sidebar "the homework assignment was to provide a list of possible solutions to the ongoing black on black and brown on brown murders within the inner city. Miss Wilson, can I get you to write the ideas down on the blackboard?"

Octavia got up from her desk and walked to the blackboard picking up a piece of chalk and an eraser.

"All right, first a few ground rules. One is to respect everyone else's opinion. And two, is to raise your hand and wait for me to acknowledge before speaking. All right, who wants to go first?"

Levitra raised her hand.

"Levitra," he said.

"I think they should have more early childhood education programs for kids from low income families," she said.

"And how will you go about creating these programs?"

JP's hand shot up. "Jeffrey."

"The government needs to spend some money on it, instead of wasting billions of dollars, starting all these wars," said JP.

"Don't you think the government has a responsibility to protect the country?" asked Tucker

"Of course they do," JP responded, "but that doesn't give them the right to play world police. I mean, the United States is always meddling in everybody else's business and can't even do a good job of minding their own."

"What kind of proof do you have to back up that statement, Mister Peters?"

"You see it on the news every day where they're over in Iran, Iraq, all over the place, but can't even fix the homeless problem here."

"Interesting observation." He stroked his chin. "Anybody else?" Levitra raised her hand.

"Levitra," he acknowledged.

"They need to have some literacy and job training programs for ex-cons re-entering society," she said.

"And how do they go about creating these programs?" he asked.

"The churches can help, so can the community centers. The school district could even have adult classes at night. And you can get businesses to start chipping in."

"Okay, I can accept that," said Tucker. "But you should know that many of those incarcerated, upon release, don't have the mental tools to take orders from someone on a job and often resort to what they know best, which is violence, when things don't go their way."

"I think you just threw every person who ever spent any time in prison into one big old stereotypical pot," stated Levitra. "That's about as bad as the police."

"Yes, maybe I did, so I stand corrected. But this class is not about what I think—it's about what you think. That's good Levitra, do you have any more ideas?"

Before Levitra had a chance to respond, the fire drill bell rang. Students jumped out of their seats rushing out of the door for what they considered an extra break. Many could be seen staring intently at their phones while others chit-chatted amongst themselves. Of course, Tucker found his way to Miss Meadow's class and knowing campus security staff, or yard teachers as they were called would monitor students conduct, kicked it with her until the students were instructed to return to class.

Back in class, Tucker resumed the conversation.

"Miss Gant, you were ready to share with us solutions you believe will fix some of the issues in our society."

"Look around," Levitra said. "Our class is half empty and this is known as an easy class."

"Easy?" Tucker asked.

"I mean colleges don't really count a Current Events class as important, Mister Tucker, but we can't even get students to come in here. We need to figure out a way to reduce the dropout rate."

"So these would be some of your solutions to reduce violence?"

"I've got many more." She held up several sheets of paper. "That's just a start."

"Okay, right now let's give someone else a chance to share their viewpoint. Who's next?" Lavelle raised his hand.

"Lavelle," Tucker called out his name.

"The police department needs to hire more than just white dudes from the suburbs who come here with negative stereotypes from the get-go" said Lavelle.

"So how would you suggest they do that Mister Brookins when the youth from your own community will not apply? You have to admit no one wants to be labeled a five-o wannabe or a sellout."

"They could start a citizen's academy where they train people in the basics of police work which opens the door for a possible career. My uncle went through the program in El Cerrito and now he's a full-fledged officer."

"Would you agree that in order to become a cop, you have to be physically fit, mentally stable, and know how to read, write, and spell? Which seriously cripples minority candidates' chances?"

JP raised his hand, so Tucker nodded giving him permission to speak.

"The process to become a cop is set up for failure if you are minority" said JP

"And your reasoning is?"

"One thing they should eliminate is interviewing your neighbors about your character because if that person is jealous, of course they'll say negative things about you. Then the cops use that as if it's the gospel without even checking out the character of the person doing the talking. Another is those mental aptitude tests. What they should require is that all cops wear body cameras on their lapels which would record everything, giving the public an honest account of police interactions with citizens."

Bobby raised his hand so Tucker nodded in his direction.

"The police need to retrain those fools on the use of excessive force," said Bobby.

"No name calling, Bobby," Tucker admonished. "We only have a minute left so hurry?"

"Okay my bad, Coach, they have to lose that shoot first and ask questions later mentality. Look at what they did to Demonte—shot him in the back."

"Anybody want to speak on that?" Tucker asked.

The class grew silent as the reality of Demonte no longer being with them returned to student's minds. Octavia handed the chalk to Levitra and sat down, as Levitra stood at the blackboard prepared to take notes from the discussion.

"I think they should follow Richmond's example and have a comprehensive use of deadly force training program to reduce the number of officer involved shootings. It's like if you use your gun, you'd better have a good reason," said JP.

"How do you know so much about Richmond dude?" Octavia asked JP.

"My Uncle is a cop there and tells me all this stuff. But back to Demonte. The cop should be held accountable for that because you're only supposed to use your weapon if your life is in danger and his life could not have possibly been in danger when Demonte was running away from him."

"Why would he rob a store when he just got a scholarship?" asked Lavelle. "The cop was trigger happy and deserves all the punishment he gets. I just hate all of the madness going on after the shooting with people, most of who don't even know him, using his murder as an excuse to steal and tear up downtown."

"Are you getting all of this, Levitra? Tucker asked as Levitra nodded and continued writing on the blackboard "Anybody else?" Bobby's hand shot up, Tucker acknowledged.

"To piggyback on what Lavelle said about the citizen's academy, they need to hire some of us into the cadet program," stated Bobby.

"I'm with Mr. Tucker on this one, Bobby," said Octavia. "They could bring it to your front door and you still wouldn't apply. Too worried about what your homies would think."

"I don't know, Tay, I mean if you join right out of high school they pay you like twelve dollars an hour until you reach the minimum age to apply to the main academy. After that, you become a real cop and if you don't make it, I heard they find you a civilian job within the department. The only catch is that you have to at least be enrolled in a jaycee to get into that program."

"Or the landscaping business," said Octavia with a straight face, everyone burst out in laughter.

"Okay no stereotyping Miss Wilson," said Tucker.

"She's not talking about lawnmowers, Coach," stated Bobby.

"Yeah, Coach," chipped in Lavelle. "She means the lannnndscaping business." The class roared their approval.

"For medicinal purposes of course," broke in Octavia. "And don't you be up there at Fresno State, trying to be no chemist either Roberto. Be done blew something up."

The bell rang and everyone prepared to leave. Tucker began straightening up the room for his next class.

"Good job, everyone," he yelled over the noise "come tomorrow prepared to talk about the lannnndscaping business," he wisecracked

The students laughed loudly as they walked out. They would definitely enjoy tomorrow's Current Events class. The rest of the morning breezed by without incident as students went from class to class. The lunch bell rang and since the students had an open campus, many left the school grounds for their favorite eating spot.

Lavelle, JP, and Bobby were joined on a courtyard bench by Levitra and Octavia. They all had chosen to get lunch from the student snack bar with their item of choice being super burritos.

"One more month and we're outta here," said JP. "Have you decided on what you're going to do?" he asked Levitra.

"I'm leaning towards the military because I can get housing and meals for free, plus get a monthly check," she answered. "They have the VA program to help you get a house and I get to travel around the world."

"They also got wars they're going to send you to and body bags that bring you home. Naw, I can't do no military," said Bobby.

"Sounds good to me, Vee," said Octavia.

"Wait a minute," said JP. "You're not going to college?"

"It's an option, but lately I've been talking to those ROTC people and the way they break it down is like you can get paid, train for a career, travel, and get an education."

"And get killed," Bobby repeated.

"You can get killed around here just as fast. Those wars have nothing on what happens in this neighborhood" stated JP.

"You got that right," said Octavia.

In the distance, the group noticed a familiar figure slowly approaching in their direction, which caused all conversation to cease.

"Hold on y'all, I'll be right back," said Levitra.

Levitra got up from the bench and walked slowly over to her sister, stopping right in front of her while staring at her in disbelief. Synnetra stared back at her twin then collapsed into her arms. The group ran over to them leaving their food on the bench.

"Taco just got killed by the police," Synnetra said breaking out in tears.

"What," said Levitra. "No, sister, what happened?" she asked. "I'll see you guys later," she said to the group.

The foursome walked back to the bench, but none resumed eating. Their attention was focused on the two sisters and wondering how did Taco get killed by police.

"Taco and T-Bone was running around there looking to get back at Blue and them for something stupid" she said "I don't know the full details but I think they shot some people before he got killed."

"Girl when did this happen?"

"A little while ago, what am I gonna do? Daddy ain't gone let me come back home," she cried.

"Girl, Daddy just mad cause you gave up school to run around with those thugs. Trust me, he'll let you come back home in a heartbeat if that's what you really want to do. You know his heart was broke when you left. You were making straight A's—Miss goodie two shoes—could do no wrong."

"I know, sister, I messed up huh?"

"Big time," said Levitra.

"To be honest, I wanted to leave but was scared Taco wouldn't let me."

"Now see, that there is what I'm talking about," shouted Levitra. "That's no way to live, being afraid. I knew you were scared of him because when I would see you, you would act like you barely knew me."

"I know, Sister, but once you get caught up, you caught up. I need to go get my clothes from his house."

"Not a good idea," stated Levitra.

"Why not, Vee?"

"Girl, if he's dead, his family is there right now turning the place upside down looking for his drug money. And if you show up and take one stitch of clothing, they'll swear you got the money while they weren't looking. Some of your old clothes are still at home and you can wear some of mine until we get you some new ones. Now what are you going to do about finishing school?"

"I never told you or Daddy, but I completed all of my requirements in December, so I'm cool."

"I thought so, because it made no sense for you to quit this late in the game. What about drugs and alcohol, you develop any habits I should know about?" Levitra inquired.

"The only habit I was addicted to was Taco" she answered truthfully. "Girl, I couldn't get enough. But I was still ready to go because the life they lived was not for me. They didn't even plan for the future past selling drugs and committing crime."

"Come on let's go," demanded Levitra.

"Where are we going?"

"Home so you can make up with Momma and Daddy."

"I don't know, Vee."

"Come on, Nee, you're going."

The twins left campus heading home. Octavia would explain to Levitra's teachers that she had an emergency and had to leave school. Synnetra felt as if a thousand-pound weight had been lifted from her shoulders.

23

INTERNAL INVESTIGATION

After learning of their immediate transfer to the Internal Affairs Division, the homicide duo of Oliver and Gutierrez cleared out their desks and took the rest of the day off on vacation leave. The change in assignment would not really present much of a problem for Oliver besides a bruised ego and maybe having to move out of his side spot. But since he and Coco were to remain partners, at least they could continue on with the affair without skipping a beat.

Oliver looked forward to working day shift instead of swing but still didn't like the way it had come about. He felt the transfer was unwarranted punishment to him and Coco, and had filed their grievance through the union. It was all retaliation coming from upper management flunkies who were afraid of the politicians in city hall, he would state to his union rep.

Coco, on the other hand, had a hard time adjusting to the move. First, she would not be able to spend time in the evenings and late night with Darnell because their hours were straight up nine to five. It was easy to tell her husband that she had to work overtime or a double shift then spend the night with her lover while on swing shift because reasons for not coming home were plentiful.

Now that time would really be cut into, because there were not too many reasons she could use to be away from home all night. Her body was already suffering withdrawal due to the time away from Darnell on the night before. She had come to regard the regular sexual encounters with him as part of her daily routine and fallen deeply in love. Knowing their time was about to be shortened hurt her emotionally.

Ironically, the main issue of overtime, which had gotten them into the mess, would not be an issue at all because IA staff received no overtime. Coco now wished they had just responded to the call and none of this would be happening. No morning commute with overcrowded freeways or nights away from Darnell.

The Internal Affairs office was housed within the Civic Center Complex, instead of inside the P-A-B for the purpose of appearing neutral in regards to police misconduct investigations. As far as the public was concerned, it was all a ruse because in their opinion, cops assigned to that unit would protect their fellow cops no matter where the reporting office happened to be located.

Situated on the first floor of the Dalziel Building right across the courtyard from City Hall, investigators were allowed a side access entrance eliminating the need to walk through the front door like the public and city employees were required to do. All investigations were conducted under a cloak of secrecy which riled citizens who fought for a more transparent city government.

The job of IA investigators to render recommendations to the Chief's office on serious matters affecting the careers of their peers was a difficult one. It was a no win situation where a decision in favor of the accused cop was viewed by the public as business as usual. On the other hand, a decision in favor of the citizen was viewed by many fellow cops as cowardice under pressure.

Darnell and Coco met outside the office at a plaza restaurant where they had breakfast before reporting for duty. The supervisor on duty was none other than Captain Nathan Johnson, father of Norman the homicide detective, and a thirty-year veteran of the department. Just as tall as his son, Nathan was a no-nonsense guy who had enjoyed a stellar career.

With only three months remaining until retirement, he was functioning on cruise control. Having worked the last fifteen in homicide, he considered that unit his own and still had a connection through his son. Naturally he knew the reason Oliver and Gutierrez were coming to his unit and frowned on their dumb decision to ignore a call out. However, true to his profession, he would treat them fairly with respect and dignity.

"Oliver, Gutierrez," the elder Johnson greeted, shaking their hands. "Let's talk in my office."

Johnson led the way to his office with them following, both wondering what, if anything had his son said about them. Their worries were unfounded because he had already been briefed on their predicament by Captain Frazier. They entered his office taking chairs in front of the desk as he closed the door then took a seat behind it.

"Welcome to Internal Affairs," Johnson spoke. "You both know what we do here and that is to investigate cases of reported officer misconduct with fairness and impartiality. Now I don't need to tell you that it's a difficult duty because in some instances, fellow officers wind up losing their jobs. My role is to make sure you investigate without favoritism because some of the cases you will be assigned to cover involve friends. Take my advice and base your recommendations on the merits of the case and not your heart. Do I make myself clear?" he asked.

"Yes, we're clear," said Oliver, "but you know we have filed a grievance and may only be here a short while."

"I'm aware of that Oliver, but until the process has run its course, I will expect you to perform your duties like everyone else," he said. "Here is your first case." He handed them each a folder. "It involves an officer you both know well, Jeremy Haskins and the officer involved shooting case from last Monday night. The list of witnesses is on the top page in your folder and most of them are scheduled to be interviewed by you two today. Do you have any questions?" he asked.

"Only one, Sir," answered Oliver.

"What's that?"

"Where's our desk?" asked Oliver.

Darnell displayed his ice melting smile as Johnson and Coco smiled with him. Johnson was happy that their meeting had went well and that they did not come in with attitudes. Leading them out of his office, he took them to theirs.

"Here it is. Let me know if you need anything."

"Thank you, Sir," said Coco.

Both she and Oliver could barely contain their joy at the shock of getting a private office with a lock on the door. They gave each other a wicked eye and laughed out loud.

"This may not be as bad as we thought, Honey," he said.

"Ooh, don't I know it," she said in a syrupy voice.

"Let's see what we got" he told her.

Their list of witnesses contained the names, address, and phone numbers of a dozen citizens, which they would interview later. On the list of cops to be interviewed today were only three, LaDarius Coleman, Robert Flaherty, and Jeremy Haskins. Coleman was already in the lobby waiting to be called, so after they helped themselves to coffee, they entered a meeting room instructing the administrative assistant to bring in Coleman.

The room was small consisting of one table with two chairs on each side of it. A large window allowing a view of the office was covered with blinds which could be closed for privacy. Oliver pulled the cord closing the blinds.

"Good morning, Officer Coleman," greeted Oliver.

"Cut the formalities, Darnell, you know my name," said Coleman.

"Have to appear professional buddy." They all smiled. "As you know, LaDarius, we're new to IA and this is our first case, so I guess we can begin by letting you tell us what you witnessed on the night in question."

"Actually, I arrived on the scene after the victim had already been shot so I didn't see that," he stated.

"Did you get witness statements from bystanders?" asked Gutierrez.

"No, I did not because I was escorting Haskins away from the scene" he answered.

"Okay," said Oliver, "what can you tell us?"

"I can say I'm not surprised something like this happened to Haskins."

"Why do you say that?" asked Gutierrez.

"You guys know that dude," Coleman said. "We would bump heads because he stereotypes the entire black community based on the actions of a few. Jeremy views coming to work as heading out into the jungle. He also he tends to use excessive force when it's not necessary."

"So you're basically a witness to his character?" asked Oliver while taking notes.

"Put it like this," answered Coleman. "I could not be his partner."

"I heard you got him out of there away from the scene?" asked Gutierrez.

"Yes, I did, Coco."

"What did he say during the ride back to the station?"

"Not one word," answered Coleman. "Not so much as a thank you."

"Well, looks like we're done here," said Oliver. "Thanks for coming in, Sir."

"There you go again." Coleman smiled.

Oliver opened the door as Coleman walked out shaking his hand along the way. He and Coco finished writing their notes and were about to return to their office when they noticed Flaherty entering the front door. Johnson walked over smiling.

"I knew Coleman couldn't help much because he was not an eyewitness to the shooting," said Johnson. "So I scheduled Flaherty's interview thirty minutes later. Don't worry, you'll catch on," he added. "It's not that much different from interrogating murder suspects where either they're lying or they're not."

Johnson walked off with those two looking at each other in amazement. Motioning for the admin assistant to bring in Flaherty, they returned to the meeting room. His interview was just as short as Coleman's had been because since he was driving the car, he was not an actual eyewitness to the shooting. As Flaherty left the interview room, he ran into Haskins, who was waiting for his turn.

"Hello, Jeremy," Flaherty greeted.

"How'd it go in there, Bob?"

"Okay, I guess. You know I can't discuss the case with you right?"

"Oh, I forgot, Mister. I'm thinking about a new partner." Haskins was sarcastic.

"Good luck, Jeremy."

Flaherty walked out the door as Oliver came over to escort Haskins in.

"Jeremy," Oliver greeted as Haskins followed him inside the room.

"Socorro," Haskins spoke to Coco, "heard you two had been reassigned to IA. Didn't know they would give you my case."

"We didn't either, but they did, so let's get started," said Gutierrez.

"Okay, Jeremy, first let me say I'm really sorry that this incident occurred and that you are in the center of it," said Oliver. "What we want is your version of the series of events leading up to the shooting. As you know, we will also interview everyone who we feel has pertinent information pertaining to the case. That's why you saw your partner leaving out."

"One thing to remember Jeremy, do not question anyone regarding this matter in an attempt to find out what we are doing," warned Gutierrez.

"May I speak?" Haskins asked.

"Sure," Oliver answered.

"On the advice of my attorney, I have been advised not to speak on this issue due to lawsuits, which have been filed by the Edwards family against me. So if you'll excuse me." He got up to leave.

"You know this won't look good on your record, Haskins," Oliver said.

"They already have me on administrative leave and will probably try to fire me just to satisfy the court of public opinion, so I don't care what it looks like, I have nothing else to say." He walked out.

"What now?" Coco asked her partner.

"We write up the report and go on break," he said matter of fact.

"You're so smart." She grinned.

"Not as smart as I'm going to be when we get off" they both smiled.

Going to their new office, they wrote up their reports then reviewed the citizen witness list. They would have to begin interviewing that group after lunch. Heading out to the plaza, they strolled around the complex, laughing and talking. Darnell reassured Coco that this would not be as bad as they had initially assumed. She smiled and did all she could not to grab his hand and hold it.

24

GRAND JURY

It was a typical Thursday morning for people jogging around, or working out at Lake Merritt. Hundreds of people were headed to work at one of the many nearby county buildings. Others waited for the main library or post office to open their doors for business. As people scurried about to their destinations, a small group of about thirty citizens drifted into a large building on the corner of 14th and Lakeshore.

They were headed for their duties as members of the Grand Jury, which met twice per week. The meetings were held in a cloud of secrecy, which did not sit well with residents who preferred more government transparency. To become a grand juror was a rather simple process where citizens from the counties juror pool filled out an application that was reviewed by one or more judges.

Nineteen people were selected for the one-year assignment with the judge having the option to allow ten from the previous year's pool to serve an additional term. There were two types of grand juries which were criminal and civil. Criminal grand jurors reviewed evidence produced by the district attorney's office to determine whether or not people should be indicted for criminal offenses.

Civil grand jurors operated as watchdog groups with the power to investigate county and local governments. Their duties included inspecting conditions in jails and detention facilities, examining books and records of non-profits or special districts in the county, and to audit financial expenditures of public funds.

The main task of civil grand juries, or the job having the most importance to residents, was to investigate charges of misconduct by public officials or employees which included cops. One of the cases they would review today was Jeremy Haskins shooting of Demonte Edwards. While the grand jury held no authority to enforce their recommendations on agencies, most complied to satisfy public scrutiny.

Two hours after the grand jury was in session, Amy Rouse rolled up with her camera crew. They parked in a red zone in front of the building and began setting up as Amy wandered into the building. Amy went inside the building, hanging around inconspicuously in the lobby until the meeting was adjourned. Shortly thereafter, juror members slowly filed out of the room as Amy did a Houdini act and disappeared.

When she reappeared outside a large congregation of citizens had assembled to receive the news of the grand jury findings. Word had travelled fast on what was supposed to be a secret, with resident's learning the outcome as just as quickly as Amy. She stood off to the side instructing her camera crew to roll the tape so she could record her report, which would interrupt midday television programs in households throughout the county.

"As you can see behind me, citizens are protesting the Grand Jury's decision not to

indict Officer Jeremy Haskins in the shooting death of Demonte Edwards. In preparation of the verdict many businesses have boarded up their windows and closed for the day hoping that when they return tomorrow, they would still have a business to come to. At the moment, police officials have not commented on the ruling but judging from the reaction of this crowd, I'm not really sure their statements will carry much weight. This is Amy Rouse reporting from grand jury headquarters."

At police headquarters, Chief Burkes and Captain Frazier stood watching Amy's newscast on a television screen inside his eighth floor office.

"What the hell was the grand jury thinking? I don't believe it," shouted Burkes.

"I would love to sit in one grand jury hearing to see what goes on. I don't understand it," said Frazier.

"How's our investigation going?" asked Burkes.

"We're recommending termination," answered Frazier. "Haskins refused to be questioned or give his account of the incident."

"Good, I'll back you on it."

Burkes lifted the television remote off his desk, punching the off button, as he and Frazier sat down to devise a plan of action for what they knew would be a night of protests, riots, and looting.

25

AT IT AGAIN

Reggie McFadden pulled up to City Hall in his midnight black BMW530i parking in the Mayor's guest stall right outside Hearing Room 3. Stepping out in a lime green suit with all the matching accessories, including a stylish Stetson brim, he walked around to the front of the building. Smiling broadly, he strutted up the front steps shaking hands of friends and strangers on the way. Turning around to face the media which had gathered for his hastily called press conference, he got right to the point.

"Once again, an officer within the police department has shot to death an unarmed black man. Some of you media folks think that since the cop who did the shooting was also black makes it all right. Well, I am here to tell you that no matter what color the cop is, it is never going to be all right. We have multiple witnesses who have given statements that the shooting was a cold blooded murder. I, for one, am sick and tired of holding these press conferences where I sound like a broken record—but if I don't stand up for the many victims murdered by cops, no one else will. The victims' families do not have the resources to fight city hall. Jakari Nelson was murdered in cold blood by Sergeant Norman Johnson and, on behalf of his family, I will be filing a civil suit against the city...."

In the homicide office at the P-A-B, Johnson and Wratney were surrounded by several detectives watching the press conference on television.

Johnson was clearly riled up by McFadden's antics along with the rest of them.

"Just give me ten minutes with that damned ambulance chaser and I'll give him a reason to sue somebody," growled Johnson.

"I wouldn't waste my energy on that piece of scum," said Wratney.

"That's not how it happened at all. Why is he lying about witnesses?" Johnson asked no one in particular.

"He'll take anybody who said they saw it, put them on the witness stand, and leave it for the Lawyer's to prove that person is lying. He's doing the same thing for the Edwards case," said Wratney. "Bringing in a ton of people who claimed to have seen it, but were nowhere near the scene."

"I don't really like that, man," Johnson said then went to his desk.

The rest of the detectives remained at the set watching furiously as McFadden continued to hold court.

"Now I encourage the citizens to exercise their right to hold a peaceful protest and advise police to allow this civil demonstration to transpire without confrontation. I also ask citizens to refrain from looting, arson, and destruction of the city."

Wratney turned the television off as the detectives returned to their desks resuming their duties. McFadden refused to answer questions from the media ending the press conference just as rapidly as he had begun it. Walking back to his ride, he got inside and eased into the flow of traffic.

26

SUMMER JOB PROGRAM

City maintenance and custodial workers busily cleaned up the Civic Center Plaza after another night of protests. The latest incident was due to the grand jury's recommendation to the city not to indict Jeremy Haskins for the shooting death of Demonte Edwards. Saturday mornings at City Hall were usually very quiet, but today was different.

The Mayor was inside the building getting prepared to address the media at a press conference organized by his office that surprisingly, had nothing to do with murder and mayhem. The purpose of today's press conference was to promote his summer youth jobs program.

Mayor Burkes stood outside his office on the landing in front of the council chambers preparing to give his annual presentation to the media about the program. He enjoyed this type of press conference because it focused on the positive happenings within the city instead of dwelling on the negatives.

Several media representatives were in attendance and had been through the routine before, which was nothing more than a glorified photo op for Burkes. He stepped up to the podium and addressed the audience.

"Good morning, everyone, as you all know, our goal is to keep the youth of this city off the streets and out of trouble. One of the most effective ways to do this is by hiring them for summer jobs, which will provide a perfect foundation for the working world in which they all will encounter as adults. We have one of the most successful programs in the nation ...."

While Burkes was boasting of an accomplishment which had been taking place long before he had ever been elected to office, his staff was busy setting up Hearing Room 4, which was located on the second floor to the right of the clerk's office. They had diagramed ten tables with two chairs on one side for themselves, and one chair for the teenaged job seekers.

Weeks leading up to the event, flyers had been posted at every junior and senior high school in the city. The line stretched from the top of the second floor stairwell cascading down throughout the first floor to the main entrance. Outside, hundreds of teen hopefuls stood waiting in a line which snaked around the corner and down several blocks. Some were joined by their parents, but most were with fellow classmates from their respective schools.

Synnetra stood patiently waiting with a group of early arrivals just outside the entry doors. As the line began to move she was allowed access into the building and ten minutes later saw a familiar face coming in her direction from the interview room. Smiling broadly, she gave him a hug.

"Don't tell me the golden boy needs money, too?" Synnetra laughed.

"Hey, girl." JP laughed, too. "Glad you decided to return to the rat race. To answer your question, I'm just trying to get an insider's look into city hall. Might learn something useful."

"Yeah, they told me you want to get into politics. What's up with that?"

"Well, they lied." He laughed again. "But from what I've been seeing since I started actually paying attention to this stuff, most politicians are on the shady side," he said.

"Way past that, dude, they be talking out of the side of their necks sometimes, saying anything they think you want to hear. Did you get a job?"

"They said they would be in contact," he answered.

"Be in contact?" she repeated. "Oh, it's my turn. Wish me luck."

"Good luck," he said. "Hey, I'll wait for you."

"Okay," she responded.

Synnetra walked inside the hearing room for her interview, amazed at the swiftness of the process. Candidates were asked five simple questions which were generic in nature, then sent on their merry way with a sheet of paper. Some people held yellow sheets while others were given white ones. She recalled that JP's sheet was white and hoped hers would be yellow.

After she went inside, JP wandered over to a few familiar faces and began having conversations with them about their status. When Synnetra returned, she was also holding a white sheet looking disappointed.

"What did they say?" he asked.

"They would be in contact," she answered. "Did you know the people holding yellow papers got hired today?" He was furious

"What?" she yelled "something ain't right. We make four point-oh grades and can't even get a funky summer job while…" She stopped mid-sentence. "Wait a minute. That's Jackie and her Daddy, who works for the city," she stated angrily.

"That dude named Elliott over there told me his mother is an Admin Assistant in the Public Works Department," said JP.

"Oh, so they're just hooking up relatives … and outsiders like us are told we'll be in contact. Nawwwww, that ain't happening. Come on, Jeffrey."

Before JP could respond, Synnetra was headed up the main stairs to the third floor where the Mayor's staff had set out a continental breakfast spread for guests. Burkes was working the area, happily shaking hands while accepting pats on the back. Most of his guests were constituents, or parents of job seekers who also happened to be city employees.

"Excuse me, Mister Mayor," Synnetra shouted. "But why is it that only people with a hookup are holding those yellow sheets of paper?" she demanded.

"Hookup?" he asked. "What do you mean young lady?" He nearly choked on his bagel.

All conversations ceased as the focus was now on Mayor Burkes and the angry young woman questioning him.

"I mean everyone holding yellow papers has some sort of connection to city hall."

"Young lady, you'll have to take up the issue with the people in charge. Maybe you didn't interview well" he said.

"Last time I looked, the sign said, 'Mayors Summer Youth Job Program' and since you're the Mayor, you *are* the one in charge," she hollered.

"Listen, I'd love to help you, but I have some important business to attend right now."

"And since we're not old enough to vote, we don't matter right?" JP questioned.

"Listen, Son," said the Mayor, clearly irritated, "not right now. I'm busy."

Mayor Burkes hurried off making a beeline to his office while Synnetra held court with the remaining guests who were acting as if they had not witnessed the heated exchange between the two.

"See that?" she spoke to the people. "He's a damned crook, that's what he is. And since I'm eighteen now, I'm voting him out of office."

"And we'll tell everyone we know to do the same," stated JP.

"I'm down with that," she said.

Synnetra and JP marched out of city hall now on a mission. Outside, they made their way down the line informing other teens awaiting interviews of the process. They explained the yellow/white paper handouts and the hook-up of city employees. Mayor Burkes watched them from his office window not worried in the least about the young black girl with her white boyfriend.

The white boy was right he thought to himself, they're not old enough to vote so they don't matter. Smiling once again, he headed back out to entertain his guests.

27

REST IN PEACE

Demonte's funeral was held on Monday morning, exactly one week after he had been killed. His family felt that the church where he had been a member, which was large, could not comfortably accommodate the anticipated overflow crowd. With an assist from Coach Tucker, the school district had agreed to let the gymnasium be used for the service.

His father, George, considered it the perfect location because it was where his son had enjoyed many accomplishments during his brief time on earth. Classes had been cancelled for the day, yet it appeared that the entire student body was in attendance. Church ushers stood in the aisles performing the same duties they would normally do on a Sunday morning, which was to hand out programs, seat guests, distribute fans, and maintain order.

The stage at the front of the gym would serve as the pulpit and Demonte's light blue casket sat on the floor directly in front of it. He lay inside, decked out in a sky blue suit with a white shirt and blue tie. Chairs had been placed on a platform directly behind the minister's for the choir, and musicians had set up their instruments and speakers next to it. They would be out of vision to the mourners which was perfectly fine with them.

There were at least a dozen floral arrangements lining both sides of the casket, which were given by school administration, the athletic department, his church, friends of the family, and parents of fellow students. As soft music played from the keyboard, people sobbed openly at the loss of their loved one. It was a wakeup call to his classmates who realized it just as easily could have been them lying there, instead of D-Money.

Three limousines pulled up in front of the gym and when family members got out, the crowd was asked to stand for their entrance. Reverend Collar led the procession flanked by ministers from his church. They were followed by Demonte's parents and sister. George Edwards wore a blue suit which was the exact replica of the one his son adorned while Karla and Kiana both had on matching black dresses with large black hats on their heads.

All three immediate family members wore dark sunglasses which failed to hide the puffiness around their eyes from crying throughout the morning. Demonte's death took a serious toll on them because it came without warning, which is the hardest death to take. They were followed by his grandparents, uncles, aunts, and cousins. Three members from his football squad joined Bobby, JP, and Lavelle from the basketball team as pallbearers and they all wore black suits.

On cue from Reverend Collar, the choir began singing a gospel song as the audience full of sympathetic friends rose to their feet facing the family. The Reverend quoted Bible passages as he slowly marched towards the stage/pulpit. Upon reaching the front, family members and pallbearers took seats which had been reserved for them by the usher staff.

Reverend Collar followed the script in the program to the letter but became slightly perturbed when the line for two minutes' tributes kept getting longer. As people would have their say and sit down, others stimulated by something they heard would get in line. Reminding the audience that the body had to be at the cemetery at a pre-agreed upon time, he cut the line off. In the eulogy, he sprinkled in many comments to the youngsters about respect, pulling up their pants, having dignity, and doing something positive with their lives.

When the service ended, a procession of at least two hundred cars followed the hearse and limos to the gravesite. Passing motorists incorrectly assumed that a celebrity had died and waited patiently in their cars at stoplights while the motorcade rolled by them. In his honor, Demonte's teammates had persuaded the school to retire his number thirty-six football and twenty-three basketball jerseys. They all felt that would be fitting closure for their fallen teammate as he rested in peace.

28

NEW DETECTIVES

Officers LaDarius Coleman and Robert Flaherty walked out of the police auditorium all smiles surrounded by family members and fellow departmental staff. They had just been promoted from officers to Sergeant and assigned to the homicide unit. Promotional ceremonies were held on a regular basis and included Sergeants promoted to Lieutenant, Lieutenant to Captain, and on up the chain. It was always a happy occasion for the ones receiving promotional status because it represented recognition for good work and came with a raise in pay.

After the reception was over and their family members went on about their business, Flaherty and Coleman, now allowed to wear suits to work instead of uniforms, entered the homicide office to cheers from the detectives on duty.

"Welcome to homicide, you guys," greeted Captain Frazier.

"Thank you, Sir," said Flaherty.

"Your timing couldn't be better. Just got a call about a triple homicide on 98th & D Street," said Frazier.

"Wow, we just got here," responded Coleman.

"Dig in, Buddy, you're rolling with the big dogs now," stated Johnson boastfully.

"Thanks, Sarge," Coleman said.

"Hey, anything you guys need ...... just ask," chipped in Wratney.

"Will do," Flaherty answered.

213

"Good job on the cases guys, did you close them all?" Frazier asked Johnson and Wratney.

"We found the murder weapon used to kill Hot Link and wound Catfish at Blue's house with his prints on it. We also found the weapon that killed Red on Hot Link's body" Johnson answered.

"Ballistics confirmed that the gun I pulled from Terrance Mayfield, aka T-Bone, was the one used to wound Blue," Wratney explained.

"The assault weapon tossed by Taco Nelson during the pursuit by Norman was turned in this morning by a citizen," Frazier gleefully stated.

"Really?" Johnson arched his brow.

"Yes, it appears that a teenager saw Nelson discard it and took it home where his parents promptly brought it to the station," answered Frazier.

"Good for them, honest people," commented Wratney.

"Have you heard from Haskins?" Frazier asked Flaherty.

"No I haven't Sir" Flaherty answered "he considers me the enemy."

"The enemy?" Johnson asked.

"If you don't agree with his jaded opinion about cultures and race, then you're his enemy. Since he was terminated, I am probably public enemy number one," Flaherty said.

"Since I was cleared, I'm probably number two," Johnson followed.

"No," Flaherty responded, "that would be reserved for LaDarius."

"Actually I'm probably more like public enemy number 1A," stated Coleman.

"You know, I can't really feel sorry for that guy," Wratney spoke. "I never liked his attitude."

"Well, he will show up somewhere else," Frazier announced.

"Why do you say that?" Wratney inquired.

"After we terminated him, an arbitrator reinstated him so he's free to sue the city for wrongful termination and get his job back if he wants it."

"Let's hope he takes that crap somewhere else," Wratney said.

"He just wasn't cut out for this city and its culture," Johnson replied. "Anybody talked with Oliver or Gutierrez?"

"They're doing okay in IA," stated his partner.

"I hate to benefit on their misfortune," said Coleman.

"They did it to themselves," Frazier told him.

"Well, I guess we'd better get started," Coleman said to Flaherty.

"Good idea," he responded.

Coleman and Flaherty left the office headed for their first murder case as the other detectives resumed their duties. They all felt that those two would fit in just fine with the unit and that Oliver and Gutierrez brought their misery upon themselves.

29

CHANGE IS COMING

The school courtyard was saturated with students enjoying their lunchtime hour. Multiple groups consisting of three to six were discussing plans for the upcoming senior prom while others ate lunch or headed off campus. For Synnetra and JP however, this was not a routine lunch break. They had staked claim to a bench table and placed stacks of voter registration cards on it, along with information pamphlets explaining the process.

Synnetra stood on the bench seat with a bull horn while JP held one in his hand too. They were on a mission to register as many eligible classmates as possible and figured where better to start than at school.

"If you want change, you have to vote" she barked into the bullhorn "you can register right here, right now.

"For those of you who did not get a summer job with the mayor's job program—you need to vote," chimed in JP. "If you want change within the police department, you need to vote. In order to get more money for school programs, you need to vote. The only way we can change society is to vote. We have to play the political game and make them understand that our voices count."

"If you are eighteen or will be eighteen, please register to vote. Tell your friends, spread the word" said Synnetra.

JP let his bullhorn rest on his hip as he spoke to Synnetra privately. Each one continued to pass out registration cards.

"I convinced Amy Rouse to cover this story and put us on the news," he said. "Our angle will be to get all high school seniors and junior college students to register."

"Do you have a plan?" she asked.

"It's already in motion," he answered. "I have commitments from every student body president at all public and private high schools along with the two junior colleges to do what we're doing. It's going to be big" he was excited.

"You really do know how to play politics. The only thing that concerns me is what if the people we sign up vote for the crooked mayor?" she said.

"We'll lead the campaign to get council member Diane Dixon elected" he stated.

"I like her—she's always doing stuff for her district. What about college?"

"Once we plant the seeds, other people will take over and I'll be off to bigger and better things."

"Cal?" she inquired.

"Yes ma'am, where are you going?"

"Cal." She laughed.

"Get out of here, for real? What's your major?"

"Political Science" she answered.

"Okay, you can be my Lieutenant Governor," he offered.

"I think you would be better as my campaign manager. Based on what you are doing right here, I'm certain of it."

"I'll tell you what" said JP "you come back here and be Mayor, then let me rumble with the big boys in Sacramento."

"I'll think about it," laughed Synnetra.

She and JP continued handing out flyers and sharing information with fellow students trying to encourage them to make a difference. Meanwhile on the other side of town, Levitra and Octavia were also on a mission to make change in their own way. The two friends wandered into the city's Human Resources Department and approached the clerk at the counter.

"Good afternoon," Octavia greeted. "We would like applications for the police cadet program."

The clerk handed them applications and they took seats ready to fill them out when Bobby walked in.

"Dude, what are you doing here?" Levitra asked him.

"I changed my mind" Bobby said.

"Yeah right, something must have happened."

"I need to make money right now to help my Mom, so I'm signing up."

"What about college?" asked Octavia.

"I just enrolled at Cal State East Bay," he answered.

"That's where we're going," said Levitra.

"It looks like we'll all be officers of the law and classmates," stated Bobby.

"What about your friends?" Octavia asked him.

"They just have to deal with it, I need to make a difference in my community. I honestly believe if they get more people who look like us, they won't have all the problems they have."

"We believe that, too," Octavia responded.

Bobby went over to the clerk and received an application while Levitra and Octavia began filling theirs out. He returned and filled his out along with them. Once completed, they all turned them in and left the building feeling refreshed. They knew that in the near future, they would be doing their part to make positive change in their community.

30

FOOT IN MOUTH

Amy Rouse stood outside Reggie McFadden's law office, unannounced, yet waiting, along with other media reps for him to arrive. They all had viewed police footage of the struggle between Jakari "Taco" Nelson and police detective, Norman Johnson. The tape they saw clearly contradicted what McFadden had been telling the public in press conferences and television interviews.

Now they wanted to hear firsthand what McFadden had to say. No one knew if he had also seen the footage but even if so, they still wanted to get his rebuttal on the incident. He pulled up curious as to why so many reporters were camped out at his place of business. Before he could get out of his car, Amy began her spiel for the evening newscast.

"I am standing outside the law offices of attorney Reggie McFadden, in an attempt to get his opinion about new evidence released in the officer involved shooting that took the life of Jakari Nelson. Mister McFadden produced several people claiming to be eyewitnesses when he filed a multi-million-dollar lawsuit against the city and its police force. However, today the police department released footage from the body camera worn by Sergeant Norman Johnson. The tape clearly shows Nelson attempting to take away Sergeant Johnson's service revolver while wrestling furiously with him for

control. Here comes Mister McFadden now."

She turned to face him as he walked up with the camera's still rolling. Several detectives in the homicide unit watched intently on the office television to see how McFadden would try and weasel his way out of this one. Johnson and Wratney were positioned directly in front of the set.

"Mister McFadden, you say you have witnesses who have given statements that the Jakari Nelson shooting was cold blooded murder. Do you still stand by that statement Sir?" she asked

"Yes, I said it." He smiled. "And we do have multiple witnesses."

"Are you aware that the officer involved was wearing a body camera which recorded the entire series of events and clearly shows Mister Nelson as the aggressor?"

The detectives let out a roar upon hearing the last question.

"BOOM!" yelled Wratney.

"The reason a lot of these guys don't want to wear a camera is because of the foul language and disrespect they display while interacting with citizens," said Johnson.

"Well, today, good, buddy, they'd better learn the camera is your friend," stated Wratney.

The detectives returned their attention to the television as smiles creased their faces. They knew McFadden would not be able to provide a suitable explanation for the videotape.

"I will have to view these so called tapes before I can comment on that" McFadden said.

Bulling past the reporters, McFadden entered his office greeting George, Karla, and Kiana Edwards whom he had scheduled a meeting with to discuss their suit. They had just watched the event outside on his office television. The Edwards family did not really care for McFadden due to the tactics he had been using in their case.

He had produced several witnesses who, according to Octavia, were nowhere near the scene. Even though they had an open and shut case against the city, George Edwards felt there was no need to fabricate evidence in order to win.

"Good Morning, family," McFadden greeted. "If you'll follow me please."

They followed him into his office and took seats while he remained standing.

"What we have is a slam dunk case against the city and we'll probably be able to get twenty million at least," he bragged.

"Excuse me Mister McFadden, but that will not be necessary," said George.

"What will not be necessary?" McFadden asked.

"A trial," George answered. "I don't want to have my family to go through the pain of all of that, reliving the tragic events which led to my Son's death. Let him rest in peace."

"I don't understand, what exactly are you saying?"

"We have agreed to a settlement offer from the city," said George.

"Why would you do that?" McFadden's voice rose. "Don't you understand that without representation they rob you blind? They'll try to low ball you for cheapest amount."

"I've made up my mind," George said flatly.

"After all the work I've done" McFadden was hot.

"We will pay your fees but no longer need your services" Karla stated.

"Just so you know, my fees are not cheap" McFadden warned.

"You can send us the bill," she said. "Thank you."

The Edwards family got up out of their seats and walked out the office without even saying goodbye. McFadden was in a rage.

"Stupid Negroes," he mumbled to himself

Outside his office, Kiana spoke to her parents.

"He'll probably charge us millions."

"Don't worry about it, child," said Karla. "The city agreed to pay his fees plus give us ten million. They said he would not be able to charge no more than one mill, if that."

"Wow." Kiana was excited. "That's a lot of money."

"We will donate some to charity, take care of our family and you, and start a foundation in Demonte's name to help inner city children go to college," said her father.

"God bless you both" she smiled at her parents.

"No, God help that greedy man in there," said George.

Karla looked lovingly at her husband who was straight-faced and burst out laughing. They got inside their car and drove to their favorite breakfast spot for something to eat.

EPILOGUE

Darnell Oliver and Socorro Gutierrez arrived for work just as a maintenance worker had finished installing a time clock and timecard holder. Looking stupidly at each other, they noticed Captain Johnson casually pouring himself a cup of coffee.

"Captain, what's the meaning of this?" asked Oliver.

"Came from upstairs" Johnson said.

Captain Johnson sipped from his mug and walked to his office closing the door. Darnell and Coco looked at each then angrily grabbed timecards with their names on them and clocked in.

"That's not fair that they could just take away our overtime like that," growled Darnell.

"And make us punch in on this damned time clock," snarled Coco.

"Maybe we should seek employment elsewhere," he said.

"Antioch's hiring," she stated.

"Let's do it," he smiled wickedly.

Darnell and Coco went inside their office and pulled up the City of Antioch's website, clicking on the link to Human Resources where they began filling out applications. At that exact moment, a large moving van travelled through Eastern Contra Costa County prepared to exit the off ramp on Highway 4 in Antioch.

Taking the Hillcrest exit, Marva Jones sat in the passenger seat as her boyfriend, Willie Crawford, drove to their new home. Tasha and her new lover, Symone, trailed behind in what had been

Blue's car with Marva and Willie's two young daughters in the back seat.

Ten miles back, another moving van was headed to the same destination. Inside it was LaDonna Tittle and her man, Derek Gatewood. Trailing behind them was Catfish, Marvette, and their four children. They would all be renting large four bedrooms, two-and-one-half bath homes on Section 8. Little did any of them know at the time, but within a matter of minutes, they would become neighbors.